D1062436

No Ceremony

John Taylor Moses

Published by RĀ Publishing Inc.

385 B Highland Colony Parkway, Suite 501
Ridgeland, MS 39157

212 White Court
Nashville, TN 37211

www.ra-publishing.com

©2004 John Taylor Moses
Editors: Jim Beatty & Andrew F. Ackers
Cover and Interior Design: George Otvos for EGO Design
Production Manager: Anna McFarland

All rights reserved. This book may not be reproduced in
whole or in part, or stored or be transmitted in any form,
without written permission from the publisher.

First Printing, April 2004
ISBN 0-9706983-7-2
Library of Congress Cataloging-in-Publication Data has been applied for.
Printed in Canada.

10 9 8 7 6 5 4 3 2 1

No Ceremony

RĀ Publishing

Nashville • Jackson

Acknowledgements

My sincerest thanks goes out to everyone at RĀ Publishing, especially Burns, Bobby Jo, and Anna. Also to Andrew Ackers in New York and Jim Beatty in Jackson, for judicious and respectful editing. I am forever indebted to the Fokas family, without whose generosity this book would have never been possible.

Note

Unless noted or written in broken English, the reader may assume that the Kefalonian characters converse in their native Greek.

For Ree

Do not let me hear
Of the wisdom of old men, but rather of their folly,
Their fear of fear and frenzy, their fear of possession,
Of belonging to another, or to others, or to God.

T.S. Eliot, Four Quartets

Maria

She swam with a grace well beyond her years. Calm. Flowing. Natural in her movements, as if her limbs were better suited for water than land.

Floating on her back she would stare up at the encompassing sky, dreaming of other islands. Other seas.

Anstice would sit on the rocks and watch his only daughter, amazed at the child's endurance. She could barely lift a full bucket of grapes, yet was able to swim for hours. He prayed for allowance, for time — so that he might witness as much of this life he created as possible. Anstice owned a café, all of his days filled with the basic reality of preparing food and catering to the tourists who came from other countries. Well grounded and able to clearly see the need for everyday tasks, he never believed his occupation meager or lacking. To him, the breaking of bread and the welcoming of strangers carried more fulfillment than any other trade. Yet the sight of his daughter swimming in the clear waters of the Ionian gave his heart a fire he thought nonexistent, her laughter an invitation to hope.

After a while he'd remove his shirt and sandals, dive into the water and swim to take Maria into his embrace. She would wrap her thin arms around his neck and wipe the water from his eyes. Then he'd go underwater and Maria would carefully set her feet upon his back, balancing her small frame as he swam slowly through the shallows, like some kind of child messiah displaying a miracle to an unseen crowd.

In the last light of day they'd walk hand in hand back to the village, shadows of the mountain Ainos stretching over the valley of wildflowers. Anstice would sing her the old songs of Kefalonia as they walked, then tell the stories behind the lyrics — her favorite the ballad that warned against any man who fell in love with an orphan girl and then abandoned her. Such a coward would be swallowed up by the sea and tormented in a great storm of waves and currents until he repented for the crime committed against the orphan girl's heart.

⤍⥊

It was the first time in a week that she'd slept during siesta — a physical and emotional cleansing. While walking along the narrow street back to the café, she finally sensed the first traces of recovery. *I suppose I get my strength from Father, his ability to emotionally endure. As if he knew more about this life than all the other souls walking around. As if he knew a certain peace, an understanding.*

Yanni sat alone in the open air of the café, smoking a cigarette, drinking coffee. He rose as Maria approached, offering a chair.

"Yassu," he said. "Did the sleep come today?"

"Yes," she said, "It came quickly and free and stayed all through the afternoon. Finally."

"I knew the sleep would come. Never give up on the sleep. Even when it goes for long time, it comes back. Always wait on the sleep."

"You don't say 'the' before 'sleep,' Yanni."

"I knew sleep would come. Like that?"

"Close. But I won't teach you anymore. I like your broken English. It endears you to me."

"Endears?" he asked.

"It creates affection."

"Ah, wonderful then," he said, "Thank you for the instruction and the no instruction. Please keep me exactly as you want me."

"Don't try to be funny in English, Yanni," she said, "It doesn't work. Only be funny in Greek."

"Nai kala Maria, oti peis." He went to the kitchen and fetched her a cup of coffee. They sat in silence, staring out at the calm sea and the outline of Zachynthos against the sky. There was no wind and the shadow of the mountain began to stretch out over the shore. Two stray dogs played chase along the beach. A man anchored his fishing boat in the shallows.

"The water's calm as oil," Yanni said.

"Yes," she said, "I love it when it's like this. It makes me want to swim for hours like when I was a little girl."

"You should," Yanni said, "You have plenty of daylight."

"Not today. Maybe tomorrow if it is calm again. What are you cooking tonight?"

"Lemon chicken and synagrida."

"Sounds wonderful," she said, rising from her chair. "I saw several cars outside of Cora's place, so there may be some new people down tonight. I'm going to walk this sleep off. I'll be back in a little while."

Yanni nodded and watched as Maria crossed the street and started down the stony beach, passing tourist children as they played in the sand; softly touching a little boy's head, as if blessing him. She took off her sandals and walked the edge of the water where shells and stones lay scattered along the shore. A long white sundress stretched to her ankles, her arms and neck dark from hours spent in the garden this last month. *I don't know if I would have made it without the garden. It seems strange that tomatoes and watermelons and field peas possess the power to heal. Something about watching their growth gave me enough purpose to live the days out. In the mornings I'd jump out of bed, get dressed and rush to the garden thinking if I didn't check on the status of the tomatoes then they wouldn't be able to live. But I had to trick myself into believing that. We need to know that things of this world depend on us. If we decide that nothing depends on our living the day, then our days don't really have to be lived, and we end up considering other fates. For so long I couldn't imagine how one could consider such an ending, but now I do. Our perspectives change like the color of trees in fall.*

I'm just glad I wasn't in Durham when it happened. Because of the clouds, Durham is only for the happy. The strong of heart. I can't imagine finding out over the telephone at school on one of those days where the clouds move low and grey and swiftly across the threatening sky. It's difficult enough battling your heart in Kefalonia where the sun arrives dependably each morning and where the olive trees grow lovely in their stony fields and the stray dogs meander without a care among the tables of the cafés. When the heart is your only foe it helps to have something appealing for the eyes.

I remember a friend at school who on Sunday evenings would flip through a collection of Ansel Adams prints. She said it reminded her heart that more glorious things existed on this earth than having a boy to love on Sunday evenings. Then she started seeing the boy from Manchester. She always loved him on Sunday evenings and never stared at the Tetons anymore. I suppose she proved herself wrong: Loving a boy on Sunday evenings may be more glorious than the mountains of the American west. I'm not sure. All I know is that the Ionian Sea is far better than the English sky when the heart feels empty.

Maria crawled up on the rocks at the end of the beach. A slight breeze rose and fluttered her dress like a flag. All the world before her was some shade of blue. The sea. The sky. The great outline of Zachynthos in the distance. She wondered how God might come to decide such a matter as color for creation, that blue seemed perfect for the sea but only because our eyes had never seen it otherwise. We truly are a vulnerable lot. I grew up believing in the certainty of always having a mother and father with the same confidence of knowing that the morning sea would be blue. So when they left me my sea wasn't blue any longer.

You and your damn sea. Why must the sea always have something to do with your thoughts? Funny how any time we want to convey the intensity of emotion we talk about seas, mountains. We paint them. We write about them. We sing about them. I think we simply love what frightens us most, and since both seas and mountains can kill us, they've become dearest to our hearts.

Yet the sea serves as the catalyst of my entire memory. I remember Father and Uncle Spiro going out on the Sunday sea to fish when I was a child. Mother and I would walk down to the shallows at dusk to see them in. They'd begin simply as a speck on the horizon, Mother always noticing them first, growing larger and larger as the light grew dimmer — their moving silhouettes against the endless backdrop of darkening water. They'd pull the small boat up on shore and Father would pick me up and raise me above his head, the sharp smell of oil and fish and salt and sweat on his hands. Spiro would immediately brag about how many more synagrida he caught than Father. Father would laugh and say that the jealousy of a younger brother never ends, then lean and kiss my mother on the mouth. She would always ask him the same question, "How was the sea?" as if he had gone to some specific rendezvous and learned its fears and hopes and who it had swallowed, who it had spared. Father responded differently each time, with soft voice, as if the sea might still be able to hear his comment, "She was as fine as she's ever been, and I've known her for a good long while."

"Even longer than you've known Mother?" I would ask.

"Yes my child, even longer than I've known your mother."

Uncle Spiro would lift the cooler of synagrida out of the boat and set it on the beach, and I would peer over the side and look at all those cold still eyes and silver slabs. I would imagine all the blue depths the fish had swam, wondering if they traveled to different seas or if they stayed in one place, just as we stayed in our village. Then we'd go back up to the house and I'd sit on the stone ledge of the garden and watch Spiro and Father clean the fish. A number of village cats always gathered on the other side of the ledge, bunched together waiting for scraps. Sometimes Father would hold me on his knee and clench the spoon in my hand, showing me how to run it along the sides of the synagrida, cleaning the scales from the tender meat. Mother would come out from the kitchen and remind Father that I was a girl and that the cleaning of fish did not necessarily have to be a part of my education. He would laugh and say that if one day I found myself on a deserted island, I would be grateful for my ability to clean synagrida. Mother would shake her head and return inside, annoyed when Father used hypothetical events that would never transpire as argument.

Maria took in a draw of breath, as if the salty air itself contained the reality of the present day and possessed the power to reclaim her thoughts from the past. She surveyed the sea another moment before starting on the path back to Katelios, singing a favorite ballad of her mother's as she walked.

Around eleven the last of the tourists left. Yanni came out from the kitchen and sat down next to Maria as she wrapped silverware within napkins for the next day's lunch. He lit a cigarette while leaning back in the chair.

"They have arrived," Yanni said.

"Yes, that was the best crowd of the season so far. It should stay fairly steady now."

"How wonderful it is that our European friends eat supper so early. By nine the rush is over and look now, the place is empty by eleven." Maria nodded in agreement.

An older couple came up the stairs into the light of the café. Maria rose without speaking. The couple took her into their arms, embracing her in silence, as if in prayer. Maria drew away and smiled.

"Yassus Yassus Yassus."

"My Maria," Mr. Kappatos said. "Would you accept our apologies for being so absent? We thought you needed some time alone."

"I will always accept your apologies, but I am fine now, so I request a complete showering of affection."

"Granted," Mrs. Kappatos said.

Yanni rose and shook Mr. Kappatos' hand. "How about some supper? Lemon chicken?"

"Wonderful."

Maria fetched a carafe of wine. Fresh bread. Tzaziki. They ate, listening to Maria talk about the last month, how she had used the garden for strength, although some of the bouts of sadness had seemed without relief from neither garden nor person nor God. She spoke of the recurring dreams she had about her childhood, mostly recollections of times spent with Father in the vineyard. Or down by the sea. Or working in the café.

"It sometimes hurts me that I never dream of Mother."

"Silliness," Mrs. Kappatos said.

"I know. I just feel like I'm leaving her out of something."

"I wouldn't wrestle with it, Maria. Your heart is waging enough battles right now." Maria nodded, staring into her lap.

"I've had a question on my mind."

Mr. Kappatos dipped his bread in the tzaziki and motioned with his hand.

"Anything, Maria," he said.

"Did my father want a boy?"

"Where did you get that idea?"

"I don't know. It's just been on my mind and I can't seem to shake it."

"Listen," Mr. Kappatos said as he ate, "You think that because your father was a fisherman and loved to work in the garden that he wanted a son to share these things with. Not your father. Your father didn't burden himself with futile thoughts like everyone else. He rose in the morning and lived the day. No motives, no secrets. Plainly and honestly."

"You know, Nouno," she said, "I don't even care if you lie to me because you speak so lovely. If lies make a girl feel this good, then I'll allow them. But only from you."

"I wasn't lying, Maria," he said.

"I know," she replied, and touched his hand, "But if you ever feel it might be better for me to hear a lie, please Nouno, lie to me."

"What you speak of is not lying," Mr. Kappatos said. "The old have a responsibility not to burden the young with things of the past that have no bearing on the present."

"He should have been an orator," Maria said.

"Please don't encourage him," Mrs. Kappatos said. "He loves the sound of his own voice quite enough."

Yanni brought out a plate of lemon chicken, tomatoes and cheese. The conversation lightened as they ate, Maria asking her godfather about the particulars of the garden, when and how often she should water the tomatoes, how to know when the Japanese plums were ripe. They asked her about the café, if she was having any trouble taking over the daily management.

"I pretty much knew everything there was to know, and Yanni filled me in on everything else. It's not so difficult. Order the food, let Yanni cook the food, be nice to the tourists. If I can pass a graduate curriculum in literature, surely I can handle this."

"It would mean so much to your folks to know that you didn't sell the place, that you've kept it running," Mr. Kappatos said, then, contemplating, "Excuse me, it does mean so much to them. I am confident that those who have left us keep watchful eyes."

"Oh, they're with me," Maria said. "Sometimes I'll be doing something around the café and I can almost hear Father's voice saying, 'Maria, Maria, my child, no, no, no, no, you must do it like this. We've always done it like this.'"

The Kappatoses nodded in agreement, as if the clarity of Maria's recounting could somehow conjure her father's voice from beyond.

They thanked Yanni for the supper and walked out into the street, Maria between them, their arms interlocked in hers. Mr. Kappatos lit a cigarette and blew a line of smoke into the night. Maria hugged her godmother and kissed the sides of her face. When she drew away Mrs. Kappatos held her by the arms.

"We wanted to ask you something, Maria," she said, "And we didn't want Yanni to hear."

Maria looked to her godfather as he stared down at the street in thought, free hand stuck in his pocket.

"What is it?"

"This is very difficult because there is no way for us to guess how you feel right now. Or when is the right time to bring things up."

"You can ask me anything, anytime."

Mr. Kappatos kicked the stones at his feet.

"It relates to what we spoke of inside," he said, "About the café. While it does fill our hearts with joy that you're running the café, it worries us that you're doing it for the wrong reasons. It's just that you'd been in England for four years with your studies and we wouldn't want you to stay here in Kefalonia out of some sense of obligation."

"I'm not," Maria said.

"Everyone must live their own life. Just because your folks never left Kefalonia doesn't mean you can't."

"This is my home."

"And leaving it doesn't make it any less your home," Mr. Kappatos said. "You have more education than anyone in the village. We simply don't want you to limit yourself."

Maria looked out across the Ionian where moonlight lay on the water. In the distance the lights of several islands dotted the darkness. "Like tired stars," her father used to say, "Come down to rest on the hillsides of Zachynthos." She thought of her time away, the things she'd missed. Weddings, funerals, celebrations, festivals, name days. She remembered coming back to Kefalonia for summer breaks, how all her cousins seemed to view her in a new light, as if she was a bit tainted from her travels. A stranger. A foreigner. She dismissed their prejudices as a combination of jealousy and ignorance, but it didn't relieve the pain it had caused. Even though her parents encouraged her to the utmost, she could never be sure that they approved of her academic desires, her longing to learn of different beliefs, different landscapes, different lives. Sometimes she questioned herself, wondering if her pursuits were authentic or simply an expensive way to separate herself from the crowd, to make her unique, special.

"There was a writer," Maria said to her godparents. "We studied him for a year in school. This man searched his entire life for something that didn't exist, some place or woman that could fill the emptiness in his chest. He traveled most every place you could think of, lived in different places for long periods of time. He wrote about the people, the land, the traditions. In the end he killed himself. I remember reading the short passages on the backs of his books that told of his life. They would mention all the different places that he lived, the different women he'd been married to, the different passions he'd picked up and then dropped along the way. There wasn't a hint of dedication or loyalty although he raised the issues many times in his texts. They would always conclude with, 'He died by suicide,' without commenting. But they were commenting, weren't they? They were commenting more than they could possibly know."

"Maria..."

"I guess what I'm trying to say," Maria continued, "Is that I'd rather know one place's soul than a thousand places' skin."

Mrs. Kappatos looked over at her husband. "The girl speaks the truth," he said. "I will accept that as your answer and say no more."

"Release your worries," Maria said, "This is where I want and need to be."

Halfway down the street, Mr. Kappatos turned and called to Maria as she went back up the café steps.

"Maria, do you remember the Morgans?"

"Your American friends?"

"Yes."

"I remember them. It's been quite some time, though."

"Their son is coming to stay with us next week. They tell us he's never been out of the States and I'm sure he'll get tired of trying to communicate with us. Maybe you could come by and speak some English with him."

"I'll be happy to."

Again, sleep — as soon as she lay against the sheets. Maria dreamt of her father; how she would sit on a stool in the café and watch him cook the chicken and lamb he'd have spread out all over the grill. Steam would rise up in his face, lines of sweat running down from his hair and across his cheeks. Often singing to her as he flipped the meat, as if working only for her entertainment.

She woke paralyzed. It was the first true night of rest she'd had in a month. Maria rose slowly and stretched the sleep from her muscles, putting on jeans and a tee shirt and walking out into the grey still of morn. The sea lay covered in shine but it was cool in the shade the mountain still provided.

She headed up the mountain road, sometimes resting for a minute, looking down into the valley of Katelios at her little house and garden on the edge of the village. She noticed how the café sat so dramatically against the sea. *So this tiny village on the southern shore of Kefalonia is where my life will unfold. I guess this is where I'll leave my mark, where I'll influence other lives, where I'll raise my family if I am dealt one. It must be the sea that makes the town look so insignificant, so unimportant. How can any single life be viewed as significant when back-dropped against the sea? The sea doesn't need us, and that's why it comes across so confident. We believe that the land needs us: to cultivate it, to water it, to alter it for its own health. But the sea perseveres without us, commanding and endless, allowing us to traverse its waters out of sympathy, pity for our helpless state. Sometimes swallowing a wayward vessel if only to remind us of its strength, its potential. It's simply immortal. Nothing can ever get to it. The sea even seems to enjoy its loneliness.*

The road flattened at Mavrata and wound through town, past the houses and the Kafenio, curving west at the church to run along the vineyards by the cliffs. The sun cleared the mountain and the hills lay drenched in green and gold. Dew sparkled across the terrain. She turned on the wildflower-lined path leading to the cemetery. A small church accompanied the graveyard, perched on a stretch of cliffs that plunged several hundred feet off into the sea.

It's a conflict of emotions, this place. Dramatic, picturesque, uplifting. At the same time, the ground in which we bury our dead. Our loved ones. Those that raised us. The people of our lives.

At the funeral the view had offended her; for every time she glanced out at the sea, her eyes couldn't deny the pleasure of the sight. She had wished for blindness that day. A failing of the senses. But those are the days where every sight is clear and crisp, every word audible. I've never felt so vulnerable. Every minute brought a new emotion, sometimes crippling. I remember being unable to stand when the funeral was over. As if my legs consciously refused. Spiro lifted me, his only niece, until I could finally stand under my own power. Spiro had lost them too, but seemed to remain untouched, emotionally above the trivial and unexplainable sadness of our short lives. Maybe that comes with years and experience, although I'm not sure if I want to be that strong. If you even call that strength. More like rigid, or simply accustomed. Spiro and Father lost their sister in the earthquake of 1953, along with half the village. I remember Father telling me the story during siesta one afternoon at the café, Spiro sitting with us and nodding to each word. He said they buried the dead from sunup to sundown for three straight days, working on the little food and water being airdropped from foreign planes. I guess after such intense despair the heart forms a shield resistant to normal, single death. Spiro's composure that day was chilling, his face devoid of any emotion, as if he didn't even know Father was gone.

At least you've gotten to the point where you can think about all this without losing it. That's good, because you're going to think about it all, over and over again. Good thing you can carry out your daily tasks as the memories come and go. I don't know if the tourists would appreciate a tear-stained hostess.

A small lean-to was built off the side of the church for funeral supplies. Maria took a spade from inside and walked down to a patch of wildflowers blooming along the stone wall of the cemetery.

She uprooted several of them carefully, carrying them through the gate and across to her parents' graves, these stone markers of lives lived. Three pictures were set within her mother's headstone, the small pane of encasing glass rattling softly in the new morning breeze coming down off the mountain Ainos. One, appropriately, from their wedding day. The second from their early years together when Mother still went fishing with Father on the sea. Taken at dusk as they approached the beach, Father standing in the back of the boat running the small motor, Mother sitting erect and proper in front as if she were a Venetian aristocrat arriving for a party. The third picture contained all three of them, Maria as a small child holding her parents' hands on the beach at Katelios, a silhouetted family staring out across the evening calm. Maria felt the tightness rise in her throat, took a breath and swallowed it confidently, then continued replanting the flowers.

She appreciated the relatives not talking openly of her mother's suicide. All had said that she simply died of a broken heart, and even though Maria and everyone else knew the truth, it was easier on the ears. Her mother told the doctors at the hospital in Argostoli to take her husband off the life support. Then she kissed him on the forehead, drove home and took twenty pills while lying in their bed. As if napping. That she already had the pills proved the consideration she'd given to her ultimate fate. Relatives took it as proof that cancer kills the victim's heart and the heart closest to it.

When Maria's work was done she stood back and looked at the grave. Such contrast, the bright flowers against the grey stone. She slapped the dust from her hands and returned the tools, headed back up the road towards Mavrata. Folks were out in their gardens now, and children passed on bicycles. She waved to distant cousins who said they'd been thinking of her. She thanked them and continued on, making sure to keep up her pace so no one could corner her. *They all want to talk about what a tragedy it was, and I don't want to hear it anymore. I know they mean well, but I don't need to be reminded about my loss. I remind myself enough.*

The bread truck rounded the corner and Maria waved it down, buying a loaf from a young man with good skin and long wavy hair. She tipped him generously and spoke her thanks.

"Tell me where you live and I'll come to your house," he said.

"I'm from Katelios," she said, "We already have a bread man in Katelios."

"Who said anything about bread?"

"Quite sure of yourself this morning," Maria said in English.

"I don't understand the words," he said, confused from her English response.

"I know," Maria said as she turned to go, shouting over her shoulder, again in English, "No boys do."

During siesta Yanni went home to nap. Maria stayed behind, sweeping the floors and washing tablecloths. Refilling the salt and pepper shakers. Cleaning the bathrooms. After four years of theoretical analysis, she found menial tasks quite rewarding. You could not discuss whether or not the floors needed sweeping. They simply did. Although seemingly meager, these small, concrete tasks carried Maria through the days of the past month; had given her focus and purpose when life itself offered nothing more than heartache and despair. To have such immediate positive results, like the night when an English lady said, "Dear, you could eat off these tablecloths," provided a sense of fulfillment when the broader pursuits of her short life — ideas, books, beliefs — only offered more doubts, more questions. Not that the craving for enlightenment had left her, rather it had been postponed until her heart could again stand on its own two feet. The poetry line, "Ignorance is bliss," hadn't meant anything until the death of her parents.

She fixed a cup of coffee and propped her feet up on a chair, staring out across the still afternoon. Downbeach tourist children played in the shallows, their laughter drifting across the water into town. The sea calm, not a breath of wind. The street empty. The stores closed. Life itself slowing to bear this hottest part of the day.

She thought back to the morning, about the bread boy, the childish pleasure obtained from a casual flirt. She'd only kissed two boys before leaving for Durham at seventeen, both distant cousins, one from Poros, one from Dilinata; neither evolving into more because there was no place to hide on Kefalonia, no possibility of a secret, youthful affair. There were too many eyes, too many cousins and aunts and uncles who would gossip their way back to Maria's parents. Even love didn't seem worth the trouble of dealing with her father's rantings about the profligate nature of boys.

When her father heard about Orcula, the cousin from Poros, he commanded Maria not see the boy again. Half teasing, yet knowing it would sting sharply, she responded, "But Father, he's such a wonderful kisser." Wounded by such an image, her father just stood there pale and expressionless. Maria became worried, ran and hugged his neck and lied into his ear, "Father, I've never touched a boy in my life, it's just gossip," holding him until the color came back to his face.

So when Keane approached her at the bar, only the second week of her life in Durham, and asked why such a good looking girl as herself wasn't sitting with a boy, Maria actually told the truth when she said, "I've never been much on boys."

"Lovely," Keane had said, sitting down, extending his hand, "I like being the underdog. I'm Keane."

"Maria," she said, taking his hand.

"I'm guessing you're not a Brit," Keane said, "The accent I mean. And the dark skin."

"Greece. Kefalonia, it's an island."

"An island girl. I like. Say something in Greek."

"Oraio paidi."

"Well?" Keane said.

"You have to earn translation," Maria said.

"Then put me to work."

She remembered how they drank beer and talked for hours, as if the only ones present, everyone else disappearing from reality, just a constant drone of chatter in the background. They left together, walking the path along the river Weir. *I described Kefalonia, told him about my childhood: growing up on an island of sun and water and rock. He hung on every word, truly caring, as if he'd discovered something precious. At least that's what I hoped he was thinking. I remember how embarrassed he became when having to excuse himself, going off into the woods saying, "That beer runs straight through me." It was such raw honesty that drew me to him, an ability to accept what life dealt, never resisting. When it dealt sadness, he wore it on his sleeve. When it dealt joy, he spread it to those around him like gifts.*

Maria remembered the unfolding from that night on, discovering and understanding this only boy of her life. How they started spending all their time outside of class together, walking along the river, taking the train up to Newcastle or Edinburgh for the day. Keane loved to golf, and she'd walk with him in the late afternoons at the public course in Durham. She would tend the pin while he taught her how to read putts. Walking the fairways, they would discuss recently read books and the ideas they contained.

Keane took a bitter stance against dreaming, said that it only got people worked up for disappointment. He believed that people who had accomplished great things or changed the world in some way probably didn't dream of such feats, only lived their life as they could and such opportunities randomly crossed their paths. Maria dissented, claiming that nothing extraordinary could be achieved unless a person's mind had been predisposed to such thoughts. Then they'd kiss, or Maria would walk clutching Keane's arm, neither of them wanting to further the argument. For they both knew, in the end, there weren't any answers to such questions.

Keane always asked if the clouds and cold got her down, since she came from a place where sunshine seemed to originate. "At first," she would say, "But not now," winking at him to hint that he was the source of her present contentment. She told him how much living in another country had changed her perspective, seeing new ways to live this life.

"It's funny," she said one Saturday afternoon, sitting in his lap by the river. "When I was a child, I thought that the world was nothing but a thousand more islands like Kefalonia, and that everyone pretty much lived the same way, only called their island a different name."

"You were a little slow, huh?" Keane said.

"I'm serious, Keane," she said, nudging his arm, "You can't grasp the fact that this life can be lived different ways until you go somewhere else."

"I know," he said, "You're right. I'd like to see how they live on Kefalonia."

"We'd have to be engaged for me to take you home."

"What?"

"It's true," Maria said, "It would cause some uproar in the village if I brought a boy home and he stayed in our house for a visit and we weren't to be married."

"What age are you all living in down there?"

"The Greek age. They tend to be set in their ways."

"Well," Keane said, "We could arrange an engagement."

"Don't tease me," she said.

I'd never possessed such an intense desire to know a boy's next thoughts. To hear his next words. Maybe I never will again.

Cole

If a stranger asked about his life, he would talk of the land. About flooded brakes in winter with the mallards lighting by the hundreds, outstretched feet and cupped wings. About dust rising up behind cotton pickers toiling endless rows of Delta fields, harvesting in late October as the timberline oaks shed their leaves of crimson and orange. About summer afternoons out on the sand bar at Moon Lake, drinking beer in johnboats and gazing at the soft brown legs of girls who came from the same land, who understood.

While prep-schooled and reared in Memphis, he left the city often, spending most weekends of his youth at the hunting camp in Mississippi, inside the levee, hunting turkey and fishing for lunker bass with all the energy his blood provided. He loved to talk of flood stages and weather fronts coming in from the southwest. His family owned cotton land in the Delta and timber farms in west Tennessee. His father managed the property. His mother painted. They begged Cole to accompany them on their frequent travels to Europe, especially the month-long stays in Greece every few years. Yet he constantly refused, always citing some game currently in season.

On Sunday nights he'd return from the camp, exhausted,

heading upstairs to his room as soon as he entered the house. Mama would follow him up, sit on the edge of the bed, ask him what he'd killed or caught. Half dreaming he'd tell her as she ran her fingers through his coal black hair. During his senior year in prep school she always wanted to talk about college, encouraging Cole to apply to several schools up east.

"I'm going to Oxford, Mama," he'd say. "It's only an hour from camp."

One time she shook her head and said, "You're gonna get lost in those woods some day."

"It'd be fine with me."

Bottomland fields stretching toward distant timberlines. Pine hills topped in red clay sand. Muddy ponds where cows drank and lay in the enduring sun of Mississippi summer. Cole Morgan studied the passing terrain as he drove east out of Oxford. He lowered the window and the warm wind came rushing up his sleeve and across his back. Merle was on the radio, singing about women and the emptiness they leave when they leave.

The road passed under him like so many before. So many miles with the wind swirling in the truck, going to hunting camps and lakes and parties out at someone's cabin, the seats always filled with laughing girls and drunken boys, coolers of beer sloshing on the floorboards. The highway had been their freedom, their youth. Their escape from the similarity of it all, the repetition of it all. This south. This Mississippi.

On the outskirts of New Albany he spotted a barbecue place. Nothing but an old commissary with a red tin roof. He pulled into the gravel lot, killed the truck, went in through the screen door. Four workmen sat in the corner, hats tilted back on their heads, sweat lines on their white tee shirts. At the counter sat a lone black man. He nodded to the boy. Cole raised his hand.

"Doin' all right?" Cole asked.

"Makin' it."

A waitress came out from the kitchen. The dirty blond hair around her ears slick with sweat, the rest all curled up and frizzy from the humidity. No makeup. Her eyes sincere. Cole noticed her hands.

"You can sit anywhere you like," she said, and motioned across the room. "I'll be with you in a minute."

He sat at the far end of the bar, tapping his finger on the countertop. He thought about Will a moment, then let it go. On the wall behind the counter were black and white photos of prize winning bulls taken at the fair in Memphis, an old Coca-Cola sign, a clock in the shape of a boll of cotton. The walls were cypress, the air smelling of wood and barbecue. The waitress came back out of the kitchen, dipped a cup in the ice maker, filled it with water, and set it in front of Cole.

"You drinkin' anything besides water?" she asked.

"No ma'am."

"You want a sandwich or ribs?"

"Sandwich."

"Slaw on it?"

"Yes ma'am."

"Some fries?"

"No ma'am."

"Quit callin' me ma'am. You're old enough to date me."

"Yes ma'am."

"I'll get your sandwich."

"All right."

She came back in a minute or two and served him. The barbecue spilled out the sides of the bun. The sauce, thick and tart, ran down his chin. He tried to catch it with his finger. The waitress started laughing.

"A napkin might help, huh?" she said, and slid him a few.

"Appreciate it," Cole said. The workmen got up from their table, stretched, came up to the counter and paid. The register rang sharply in the room as it opened and closed. Cole ate his sandwich. After a few minutes the black man rose, laid a few dollars next to his plate and nodded to the boy.

"Have a good un'," he said.

"You too," Cole replied.

"See you Monday Sandy," the black man called back to the kitchen.

"All right, Leroy," she called back, "Don't work too hard."

"You ain't got to worry 'bout that," he said, the slap of the screen door confirming his departure.

The room was still now, random noises coming from the kitchen as the girl worked in back. Dust hung in the dim shine

that filtered through the shuttered windows. A radio clicked on
in the back room, and Cole recognized a familiar country tune.
He sang the words in his head as he finished the sandwich. The
waitress came through the swinging doors.

"You like country, don't you?"

"Yes ma'am," Cole said. He wiped his mouth and put the
napkin on the empty plate, sliding it across the counter. She took
the plate and dropped it in a dirty dish tub. She pulled a stool up,
sat, took a pack of smokes out of her pocket and laid them on the
counter. She lit one, dragged off it and blew a thin line of grey
toward the ceiling.

"Want one?" she asked.

"No thanks," he said, "Never started."

"Good for you. My name's Sandy."

"So I heard. I'm Cole."

"Nice name."

"Thanks."

"You ain't ever eaten in here before, have ya'?"

"No ma'am, I'm just passing through. I live over in Oxford."

"You go to school?"

"Did," he said. "Graduated in May. Just haven't found a
reason to leave yet."

"I like Oxford, too," Sandy said. "I go over there with my folks

some on Saturday's to eat lunch with my aunt. Mama and I go
up to the Square after we eat and window shop the stores."

Cole nodded. Sandy smoked.

"Where you headed?"

"Tupelo today," he said. "I'm going a bit further tomorrow."

"I see."

They sat in silence a moment, both staring away from each
other. Cars could be heard humming past on the highway. Sandy
finished her smoke, crushing it out in the tray.

"You want anything else?" she said.

"No ma'am. I better get on."

"All right," she said.

Cole took his wallet out, started counting bills. Sandy picked
up the tub of dirty dishes and started for the back room.

"Take care, okay," she said. "Have a safe trip."

"What do I owe you?"

"Nothing. First sandwich is on the house. Come back and
see me sometime."

"But..."

"But nothin'," she said, "Now get on." Cole watched as she
disappeared through the swinging doors.

Soon he was on the old two-lane again, flying past clapboard
houses and mobile homes that sat anywhere some trees had been

cleared away, atop pine knolls and along creek banks, cars parked in the grass, tricycles and swing sets and lawn mowers adorning the yards. A lady in a pink tank top smoking a cigarette leaned on the hood of an old pickup, watching her little ones play in the dust. In the midst of her day, her life. *Maybe she's got a good man out working construction or scouting timber, a father to her kids, a man that takes care of them. Probably not. She probably ain't got a clue where supper's gonna come from.*

Cole drove on.

He passed stands of old growth in some of the bottoms where he could look through the big oaks and see for a hundred yards. Untouched timber blocked the sunlight from the forest floor, keeping it clean and shaded and cool, easy for a man to walk even in the heat of Mississippi summer. He traveled through a stretch of high ground scoured by clear cutting, a tangled growth of buck brush and baby pine and head-high sagegrass that Cole knew held bobcats and bedded-down deer. Copperheads that could kill you dead. He'd heard snake stories from the foreman of a timber crew that worked Mississippi and Alabama during the hot months; stories he'd never heard the likes of and wouldn't want to again. Size of your damn calf, the man had said. Moccasins with mouths the color of snow. Keep a man from sleeping nights.

He reached US 78 and hit it running, past rickety trucks

filled with day-laborers and eighteen wheelers driven by men with hard faces and squinted eyes, men who only nodded when Cole raised a wave. The hot wind across his face, the taste of sweat on his lip. He hadn't ever been much on running the air, didn't like anything to separate him from the day. Wanted to accept all it offered, even if that included ninety degree heat. *But you didn't want to accept what May 26th brought Will. He didn't deserve it. Me or Smitty, yeah, we probably deserve a comparable end. But not my boy Will. Life ought to have showed more respect to someone who possessed such a blind trust in its promise of future.*

Try to think about something else, Cole, something easier on the heart. Think about Lily, how she used to come up behind you at the bar and put her arms around your waist, whispering as her lips swept the back of your neck, "Let's get out of here." And you'd just nod and take her hand, wouldn't you bud, not saying goodbye to anyone, sometimes not even closing your tab, as if leaving this life, walking home through the quiet, dark streets. Sometimes pulling her up under an oak in a strange yard and kissing for a good long while, because you could, because you were young and you knew the good things that were going to happen when you got back to the house and you wanted to put if off a little while because the anticipation of doing that with her was almost as good as the doing.

It went fast, didn't it old bud? As if you were aware it had to end the whole time it went on, like a carnival ride. I guess that's how it goes. You pay your money and ride as long as you can. It just doesn't seem fair that you had to meet her with only one year left of school. Live in the same town for three years and cross each other's path with only one to go. Just long enough to see what you'd been missing and then have it snatched away.

She looked striking at the funeral. I didn't think she was going to come all that way. It was hard, too, so soon. Said goodbye that Sunday afternoon after graduation, said it for good. And only three weeks later she comes back for the funeral and we had to do it all over again. At least you got one more night with her. You felt awful about it, laying Will to rest that day and being with Lily that night; it somehow seemed irreverent. But you don't even want to think how hard that night would have been if she hadn't been there, in the crook of your body, all warm and kissing your back and telling you over and over again that you couldn't have done anything to stop it, that some things happen just to prove that this life makes no sense at all. And then, after a long silence, she whispered her news: "I won't be in the south again for a good long while. Maybe never, Cole."

Smitty's driveway was lined with big oaks that shaded the gravel and let piercings of light trickle down through the leaves. Cole pulled up next to the house, killed the truck. Smitty's mama was sitting on the screen porch reading a magazine. She rose and came out, letting the door slam behind her. She put her arms around Cole as he exited the truck.

"Oh, Cole, I've been thinking about you boys so much. Can't imagine what you've had to go through this last month. Are you doing all right?"

"Yes ma'am, Mrs. Cook. I'm doing fine, considerin'."

"Yes, yes, honey, considerin'," Mrs. Cook said. "I guess that's all we can do."

She led him to the house, holding the back of his arm. In the kitchen she poured him a Coke and sliced him a piece of pound cake. Cole ate and nodded to everything Mrs. Cook said. She talked about Will, what a shame it was. Cole nodded some more.

"Smitty told me you might stay with us a night or two. I wish you'd stay several days. Smitty seems lonely these days, Cole. He never talks and when he gets off work he just goes down to the lake and fishes until dark."

"Well that doesn't sound too strange to me, Mrs. Cook. You know if there's daylight left then Smitty's gonna be fishing."

"I know, but still, something about the way he carries himself now. Why he doesn't even tease me anymore, and you know how much of a kick he used to get out of rowling me up. I just wish you'd stay a few days and talk to him."

"I would, Mrs. Cook, swear I would. But I've got to catch a plane in Atlanta tomorrow night. And besides, Smitty's probably like me. He prefers silence to a bunch of endless talk."

"Maybe you're right. Maybe I'm just rushing him to get over it. Oh well, anyway, I forgot about the trip you were taking. Smitty mentioned something about it. Said your folks thought it would be good for you to get away for a while. I think it's a good idea."

"I guess," Cole said. "They insisted that I go, and I wasn't much in the arguing mood."

"Well, you'll be better for it. Get you away from all the reminders. Anyway, go see Smitty. He's down at the lake."

"Yes ma'am." She walked over and opened the back door for him, patting Cole's shoulder as he passed.

"Y'all come back up to the house 'bout dark. Mr. Cook's gonna grill y'all some steaks when he gets off work."

"Yes ma'am."

Down through a small patch of kudzu woods, through an old

gate, up over the top of a grassy hill and then the small lake with
its sunken pine trees and cypress stumps — Smitty skulling in
a johnboat with his cane pole and jig. Cole sat on the bank
and watched him a moment, admiring the concentration that
possessed his friend.

"If you paid a girl half the attention you pay those crappie, you
might not be such a lonely son of a bitch," Cole called from the bank.

"Hey Cole Morgan."

"Hey Smitty Cook."

"Hang on," Smitty hollered, "Let me come get you."

Smitty set his rod down and paddled over to the bank, a small
black wake splitting the water behind him. He swung the back of
the johnboat toward the bank and Cole crawled in. They looked
at each other.

"Well," Smitty said.

"Well what?" Cole asked. "Hand me that other rod and let's
get to work. I've got some catching up to do." Cole could hear a
mess of fish flailing around in the cooler. "How many you got?"

"More than you could ever catch," Smitty replied.

"Shit, here we go."

They fished a group of sunken pine trees, each picking up a
slab here and there, rowling each other when the other caught
one. They talked about how hot it had been, how low the river

was, how Smitty's job at his uncle's lumber company was going.

"It's gonna be a good deal," Smitty said. "You know I ain't gonna live anywhere but Tupelo. With my uncle not having any kids or nothing, I'll probably be able to take the place over when he retires in a couple of years."

"That's good," Cole said, "I'm happy for you, bud."

"You still writing some?"

"Yeah," Cole said, "But not as much lately. Since Will."

"I hear you," Smitty said.

"But I feel worse when I don't write, so I try and keep at it. No reason to quit and no real reason to keep going. Stuck in the middle I guess."

"Well," Smitty said, "Just keep doing it. You ain't got anything better to do. Seems like there's a lot of time to occupy these days. You know, it used to piss me off something terrible when we lived together our sophomore year and every night around eight you'd disappear into your room and write 'til midnight. And I'd sit out there like a bump on a log watching television."

"You should've gotten you a girlfriend," Cole said.

"I ain't never been any good at that either."

"Just as well," Cole said, "All they do is take you to a level you've never been then leave you a rung lower."

They fished a while in silence. A south wind picked up and

rippled the black lake water. Turtles splashed off logs as they
sculled past.

"You miss Lily?" Smitty asked.

"Yeah."

"You think about Will?"

"All the time," Cole said. Cows were grazing up on top of a
distant hill and the fields lay green and brown. The sun eye-level,
shadows stretching farther out across the lake. A mosquito
buzzed Cole's ear and he slapped it against his neck.

"Those y'all's cows?" Cole asked.

"Naw. Dad rents the field out to an old codger down the
highway. He's got about fifty head out here." Cole nodded.
"Cole?" Smitty said.

"Yeah."

"When we crawled out of the truck and saw..."

"Smitty?"

"Yeah."

"Let's not. I've done it to myself too many times lately."

"All right," Smitty said.

They ate supper on the screen porch, crickets sounding. Mrs. Cook did most of the talking, asking Cole questions about girls and plans for the future.

"Sally, would you let the boy eat his steak," Mr. Cook said abruptly, and Mrs. Cook fell silent a moment, grinning with embarrassment.

After a few minutes she said, "Tell us about your trip, Cole."

"I fly out of Atlanta straight to Athens," he explained, "Then I catch a little puddle jumper over to the island."

"My heavens," Mrs. Cook said, "I've never even been out of the country. I'd be scared to death. How do your folks know these people?"

"They honeymooned on the island," Cole said, "And met this young couple while they were there. Ended up becoming great friends and have stayed in touch ever since. I think Dad and this man do some business. They go over every couple of years."

"Good Lord," Mrs. Cook said, "Jim and I here honeymooned in Gulf Shores, Alabama. You blue-bloods are too much for me."

"Sally," Mr. Cook said, "Would you please not embarrass the boy?"

"Oh I didn't mean it like that. I'm just kind of overwhelmed by it all. I mean, he's talking about going to Greece as casually as I'd talk about going to Hattiesburg. I'm sorry if I'm being silly."

"No ma'am," Cole said, "I'm kind of overwhelmed by it all myself. I've never traveled like my folks. They're just kind of making me go this time."

"Well, it's a good thing to do," Mrs. Cook said, "Get to see a new place like that. Take your mind off everything that's happened. I wish Smitty would go somewhere."

"Mama," Smitty said.

"Well I do. You deserve a break from everything."

"Stop it," Smitty said.

"What's the name of the island?" Mr. Cook asked.

"Kefalonia."

"That's just beautiful," Mrs. Cook said.

"You and your drama," Smitty said. "I enjoyed it, Pop. Those steaks were perfect. You done, Cole? Let's go riding."

"Yeah, I'm done," Cole said, sliding his chair out. "I enjoyed it, too, Mr. Cook."

"Wait now," Mrs. Cook said, "You sure you boys got enough. There's more of that pound cake. Why don't you let me cut y'all some pieces?"

"We'll grab a piece before we hit the hay, Mama," Smitty said, taking his keys out of his pocket and opening the screen door.

"Don't y'all wait up for us."

"You boys be careful," Mr. Cook said.

"Yessir."

"Yessir, Mr. Cook, we will," Cole echoed back.

A Mississippi summer night like the ten thousand others they'd lived, the headlights illuminating a road corridored by kudzu and big oaks and tupelo gums, a creek bridge every now and then. The smell of rich bottomland riding the wind. Along fields they could make out the golden eyes of deer standing still and true, their figures silhouetted against the moonlit bean rows. Coons scurried into culverts as the headlights exposed them. A dead dog lay in the shoulder gravel.

Across the county line Smitty stopped at a beer store, a tin building with a windowless door, a lone white spotlight shining across the lot. Cole stayed in the truck, thinking about Lily on Sunday afternoons in the fall, when the days started getting a little shorter and the air took on a touch of sharpness. The light from a lingering sun would stretch across October fields of cotton all white and full, riding the highway out to Sardis Lake, Lily talking about her plays and how much she wanted to be an actress. *She'd sit with her back to the door, legs crossed in the seat, facing me, going on and on about how much power an actress has over the world. More than an actor, she'd say, because a woman's heart is deeper than a man's, and therefore can evoke more compassion, sympathy. She'd talk the whole ride out to the lake, and then, when I'd pull the truck up on the sandy beach and kill the engine and the little muddy waves would start lapping against the shore, Lily would fall silent and look out across the murky water and say, "We're here." "Yeah, Lily," I'd say, "We're here." Then we'd kiss for a good long while. Come sunset we'd drink a few cold beers on the tailgate and watch the day end, the sweet beer making the words come easy and true until darkness sent us home to sleep Sunday away.*

"What ya' thinking about so hard?" Smitty asked as he climbed back in the truck, laying the wet sack on the console and cranking the engine.

"Nothin'," Cole said.

"Sure."

Smitty pulled out of the lot and went on down the road, passing an old pickup along a stretch of flat. He took his smokes out and pushed in the lighter, retrieving it and cupping his hands on top of the wheel. He dragged off it and looked over at Cole.

"Listen man, are you gonna pop me a beer or do I have to get one myself?" Cole pulled two beers from the sack.

"Appreciate it, bud," Smitty said, raising his can to a toast. Cole tapped it and took a pull, then hung his arm out the window and stared at the night.

Smitty turned back towards Tupelo, driving faster now with

his beer between his legs, palm outstretched into the wind. They rode in silence as they approached town, past the gas stations and darkened stores, both staring out at the world as if looking for something in particular — something they could recognize as what their eyes were searching for. Smitty wheeled down Old Lake Road and gunned the accelerator.

"Macy Fisher said something about coming by her lakehouse," Smitty said, "Might as well check it out."

"All right."

"Hand me another beer, will ya?"

"Yassuh, Mr. Cook."

It was a good ten minutes out to the lake, the road topping the low hills with the cow pastures all white and hazy in the half-moonlight; the truck headlights illuminating silver field gates with no trespassing signs as the boys sped on. Past the old lake store and a row of cabins, folks sitting on their porches enjoying the summer evening.

Smitty pulled into Macy's drive behind an MG convertible. He killed the lights.

"That's Macy's old man's ride, but she drives it all the time. Come on, let's see who's here."

Cole grabbed the few beers left in the sack and followed Smitty down to the cabin. They could hear girls laughing on the porch so they walked around the side yard and came up out of the darkness into a spotlight that shone off the back of the cabin. It was dark on the screen porch and Cole couldn't see any faces, only the flaming embers of cigarettes and the tin flash of beer cans. They stood in the yard light like two thieves caught in the act.

"Why Smitty Cook," a voice said from the porch, "You've found a friend."

Smitty smiled and opened the screen door. Cole followed. On the swing sat two girls.

"Cole my friend," Smitty said, "This is Macy Fisher and Kara Young. They've known me as long as my mama has."

"I'm sorry about that," Cole said, giving them both his hand.

"Y'all stick that beer in this cooler," Macy said. "We got plenty if y'all run out." Cole dropped the beers in the cooler, sitting down in a wicker rocker next to the swing. Smitty sat across from him; lit another smoke. "What y'all been doin'?" Macy asked.

"Mama fed us and then we got some beer and just been ridin'."

"Sounds like fun," Kara said.

"Cold beer and country roads," Smitty replied.

"I'll drink to that," Cole said.

Kara nodded. Cole watched her.

"What about y'all?" Smitty asked.

"You're lookin' at it," Kara said.

"Well," Smitty said, cracking a new beer, sipping from it and sighing, "Shall we begin?"

They talked about the end of school. What to do now that it was all over, this existence as students they'd been living for the past fifteen years. Not a simple transition, Cole added. The conversation unfolded naturally, filled with youth, sincere. The alcohol gave it all a sense of importance, as it always did, that the words being said held value, truth. Old enough to be out of school yet not old enough to make the real decisions, or at least wishing the real decisions would hold off a little while longer. The beer went down like candy, laughter at each story.

Cole caught Kara's eye several times, both holding the gaze, daring each other to release it, the potential of something unknown brewing as the conversation unfolded. *Lily's gone, bud, there's nothing noble in preserving that which is gone. And this Kara girl is easy on the eyes.*

Hours passed. They finished the beer and Macy fetched a bottle of her old man's whisky from the basement. They mixed it with water and ice, the liquor biting as it went down, flushing their faces, eliminating all knowledge and belief of the tangible world which transpired during the week.

After a while Kara whispered to him, "Listen, you wanna walk down on the pier?"

"Love to."

"Come on," she said, then turning to Macy, "We're gonna sit on the pier a little while."

"Go sit on the pier," Macy responded, "Me and my old friend Smitty will hold the fort down."

They rose and went out through the screen door, across the lighted yard. They went along the cypress-planked walkway out to the dock — Kara in front, Cole following, a slight south wind rippling the black water out across the lake. Cole watched her braids bounce back and forth off the small of her back as she walked, imagining what her hair would look like free and down, or spread out over her body as she slept. All of a sudden he felt the urge to touch her, to kiss her on the mouth, to brush his face across the flat part of her upper chest. It was the first time in a long while he'd felt such an emotion for any girl besides Lily, and even longer since he'd actually touched another. *I'm gonna have to learn how to do this again. Lily's gone. For good. Some things in this world are for certain and one is that you're not going to spend your life in Boston. And she is. So just think about this girl named Kara and let the night unfold as it should, and don't let that drama with Lily get in the way. Lily's probably with someone else by now anyway. No, you know she is. She's too striking to go unnoticed, and she's got too romantic of a heart to go without love. You can't have everybody, bud, so just live this night dealt to you and don't worry about what you can't control.*

Kara sat down on the bench railing, pulling her knees up to her chest as if she could be cold in Mississippi summer, lighting her smoke and wrapping her arms around her legs, resting her chin in the little crook between her knees. Cole pulled up a wrought-iron chair and propped his feet up on the railing next to her. She smoked and Cole stared off at the black timberline on the far shore of the lake. After awhile Kara motioned towards the water, the steady flicker of moonlight.

"I love that light," she said.

"Yeah."

Kara took the last drag off her smoke, flicking it over the edge of the dock.

"I heard what happened to you and Smitty's friend," she said. Cole sipped from his whisky and didn't look at her. "I can't imagine how hard that must have been. Actually being there. Happening like that."

Cole nodded and stared down at his lap. "Yeah," he said. Moments passed. The wind stirred the trees up by the cabin. In the distant sky he could see a line of black clouds creeping across the stars.

"Might be a storm blowing up," he said, motioning with his head. Kara stared at him curiously. He caught her eyes, then spoke: "The hardest part is accepting how stubbornly life goes on. I wanted everything to stop. I wanted the world to quit eating and quit sleeping and quit working. Doing anything except thinking about it seemed inappropriate. But the world didn't stop. Nothing stopped. You have to get up and eat breakfast the next day and take care of whatever needs doing. And you run into people and maybe even share a laugh about something, and afterwards you get in your truck and say to yourself, you son of a bitch, one of your best buddies just passed on and you're sharing a laugh with somebody. It kills you. You hate yourself for doing normal things like getting hungry or playing with a friend's dog. But you can't stop yourself from living. You have to live the day. And you lie in bed at night and apologize to him for living and then you get up the next day and live again. You don't have a choice. What's hard is knowing that you're gonna be all right, that you're gonna get over it. You feel like you owe it to him not to be all right."

"What was his name?" she asked.

"Will."

"Thank you," she said.

"For what?"

"For telling me all that. You didn't have to."

"Well," Cole said, "Sometimes it's easier to tell a stranger than someone close to you."

"Am I a stranger?"

"You were an hour ago," he said.

"Am I now?"

"I don't know. You don't look like a stranger."

Kara smiled. "Can you make friends that fast?" she said.

"What do you think?"

"I think so."

"Me too," he said, taking a last pull from his whisky. *Well, go on. Get back on the horse. She's lovely, and if there's such a thing as true loneliness you've felt it these last weeks.*

Cole rose and gently pushed Kara's legs down off the railing. She sat watching him in the half-dark.

This boy, this girl — trying to accept the ways of their own hearts, not questioning why they feel the way they do but rather simply believing that there could be a purpose to this emotion, this desire to touch one face to another, knowing that the evocation of such longing comes not completely from the skin, but from some void or vacancy that if filled would allow them sleep in the night and fulfillment in the day. Running his hands now across the tops of her blue jeans, his chin lowered watching his own hands yet moving ever closer until his cheek alongside hers, Kara whispering, "I don't know why I asked you to..." and he silencing her with "It doesn't matter," now brushing his cheek against hers and Kara lifting her hand to the other side of his face, holding it as if he was hurt, as if comforting him from some sudden and terrible loss. Kissing her cheek once and then the side of her neck once and then rising and taking her thin warm lips inside of his, slowly and quicker then slowly again, there being no time now, only this true and indefinable presence; Kara placing her arms around him and running her fingers across his neck, birthing the impossible yet confident thought in Cole's mind that he has known her for a very long time.

And the rain coming so softly at first that they don't even feel it, or simply choose not to. Then thunder and sheets of cool summer rain sweeping across the lake in waves. Cole and Kara running back to the cabin along the cypress planks.

The road home was barely visible through the summer storm. Pockets of muddy rainwater collected along low spots in the road. Cole had to hold the wheel firmly with both hands to keep the truck between the lines. Smitty and Macy had gotten deeper into the whisky, and Smitty riding shotgun dozed in and out of a drunken sleep.

A mile or so before home, Smitty started to shake. He wrapped his arms around his chest, as if trying to embrace himself. His sobs silent at first. Cole reached over, setting his hand on Smitty's back.

"Smitty, hey bud, what the hell? What's wrong?"

"I told him, Cole, I told him to do it."

"Told who to do what?"

"I told him. It was me. You remember. I'm the reason he ain't here. I made him do it. You remember. I told the son of a bitch he couldn't hold his liquor."

"Oh Jesus, Smitty. You can knock that off right now."

"I told him, Cole. I told him. I told him that he always made us drive. I made him feel bad. I told him. It was me."

"Stop it Smitty."

Cole turned into Smitty's drive and eased down the gravel under the big oaks still swaying in the wind and rain.

"All right now Smitty, we're home. You've gotta straighten up. What happened isn't your fault and you've got to get that through your head right now."

"I told him. I was the one. You even said that you'd drive. But no, I told him he needed to drive. I told him he hadn't had as much as us. I knew he couldn't hold it like we could. But I told him. I told him. I knew he couldn't hold it like we could. Shit, I'd known since the day we met our freshman year. I should have driven. Me or you. Like always. But no, I just wanted to ride and drink some more so I made him feel bad. I told him he needed to drive."

Cole pulled up to the house, dark save the light on the screen porch.

"C'mon Smitty, let's go to bed. It's just the whisky talking. That whisky's got you all tied up."

"No," Smitty said, "I told him. I told Will to drive."

The song on the radio ended, followed by a moment of silence, then the clean guitar lead to the Allman Brothers' Blue Sky. The rain poured down the windows, the distant sound of thunder. Every moment or so the world would brighten briefly with lightning. Cole reached over, placed his hand on Smitty's shoulder. As the song continued Smitty's sobs lessened, fading to silence until he gathered himself and wiped his face with the sleeves of his shirt. Both looked ahead at nothing. The guitar solo sounded through the speakers, then the final verse; the DJ's interrupting voice tarnishing the last notes of music. Cole turned the radio off. They sat quiet for several minutes listening to the summer storm, the rain on the hood.

"Finest guitar solo ever played," Smitty said after awhile.

"No question."

"Bring a man to his knees."

"Or off them," Cole said.

Smitty leaned on the hood of Cole's truck and stared at some unknown point on the morning horizon. Cole stood next to him, one foot resting on the fender. He sipped his coffee.

"Well," Smitty said.

"Your mama fixes a mean breakfast."

"Yeah she does," Smitty replied. He spat into the yard. "I don't know why it hit me last night, bud."

"Ain't worth talking about," Cole said.

"Nope, you're right."

"Whisky brought him back to you."

"Yep."

"It'll do it. Old Will liked to take a sip himself, didn't he?"

"Yeah," Smitty agreed. "What'd he used to say? 'The money's gone and the mind is shot but the whisky we still got.'"

"Something like that," Cole said. "I guess I better run."

"What time you fly?"

"Late afternoon."

"What the hell's Greece gonna be like?"

"You know as much as I do," Cole answered.

"You nervous?"

"Kinda."

"You ain't missing anything here," Smitty said. "Fish almost done biting. Dog days aren't far away."

"Yep."

"Wonder what you'll do while you're there?"

"I don't know, bud, but I guess I better go find out." Cole tossed the coffee dregs into the yard.

"You ain't nothing but a little rich boy, you know. Flying to Greece, I swear."

"You know better than that," Cole said. He crawled in the truck, cranked the engine, lowered the window. "Listen, tell that Kara girl she may not have seen the last of me."

"You need to shake Lily 'fore you start cattin' around again."

"I ain't studyin' Lily."

"Sure you aren't, heartbreak. Don't think I didn't notice you two slipping off after the funeral."

"That's low, bud."

"Hell, Will would of wanted you to get a little love on account of him. He probably considered that an honor."

"Try not to think about him, hear Smitty?"

"Ain't no prayer in that. But I'll be all right. I'm just waiting on time now. Need a little to pass. You go on, rich boy."

"Hold the fort down while I'm gone," Cole called as he started down the drive.

"Always," Smitty hollered back.

May 26th: *The first days of Mississippi summer with the bottomlands all full and lush, cotton beginning to show in perfect rows. The smell of honeysuckle along fence lines; blacks fishing for bream off the sides of creek bridges. These boys Cole and Smitty and Will just three weeks out of school and no decisions made, life still an endless succession of where folks were going to be any given night: up at the bar on the Square, out at Jimmy Bogen's lake house, down on the beach at Clear Creek. Their skin already dark from afternoons fishing Smitty's farm lake outside of Holly Springs; their hearts trying to hold on to a youth that seemed to slip with each passing day. That Saturday Fletcher calling them early, waking Cole with the news that a crew of girls from Clarksdale was spending the weekend at Moon Lake. He had been drinking with them last night over at Jenny McIntire's cabin. As fine a crew of girls as any boy could ever dream of assembling, Fletcher said.*

Tearing out of Oxford as soon as he could get Will and Smitty roused and showered, stopping at Rick's Store just past the county line to fill their coolers with ice and beer, Smitty taking his first pull from the can, leaning his arm out the window, thrusting his fist in the warm wind and pointing his finger toward the high, midmorning sun. Cole turning up a Willie album and the boys singing Pancho and Lefty as if they'd wrote it themselves. The yellow dashes of flat highway passing under the truck forever and always, the next no different from the last except to bring them a little closer to girls and water and boats, terms that could characterize as much of this day as these boys wanted to know. Life to them an endless promise of future — to always deliver summer days of good friends and cold beer so that they might build an infinite collection of memories that no hurt or sorrow could ever match.

Through Batesville and dropping off into the Delta, a hazy fume of white sunlight lingering over the land, lone oaks standing defiant and enduring in distant fields where turnrow meets turnrow. These boys watching the rows of beans and cotton dart away from them as they pass, saying little now, drinking their beer and listening to the twang in Willie's voice; over the Coldwater River and through the stop at Marks, heading west on the potholed county road to Jonestown. No change in the landscape. No field distinct from the other. No bayou without the same muddy water and the same haunting cypresses. Past the store in Jonestown, black children playing hopscotch in the parking lot and young stout men leaning against cars and drinking malt liquor from quart bottles wrapped in brown paper sacks.

Minutes later crossing US 61, following the last miles to the dead end at Moon Lake, trucks crowding the lot at the store, fishermen buying minnows and jigs and beer and pork rinds. Turning along the lakeshore toward Fletcher's cabin, pulling in and killing the truck, carrying the cooler out to the dock, Fletcher sitting in the midst of six Delta girls taking in the sun. Will whispering to his partners, "I like the odds."

The afternoon unfolding same as always, the hours passing toward dusk without distinction, nobody considering time. Fletcher grilling ribs for lunch and then everybody crowding onto his pontoon boat, heading out to the sandbar where several other crews of young people were anchored, drinking and swimming in the shallows. Will paying particular attention to Mimi Reston.

The alcohol causing the entire scene to blend together like water on a fresh painting, until the day becomes an unclear yet striking memory of skin and water and laughter. Sunlight going down over the levee. The sky changing from white to a lesser violet, Fletcher saying that it was time to head back and Will and Mimi climbing up into the back of the boat from where they'd been kissing and talking in the water. Cole riding on the front between Halle and Mary, his arms around them, explaining how lucky they were to have so many semesters ahead, innocence still in their pocket. A fine mist of lake water spraying their dangling legs.

Back at the cabin everyone saying their goodbyes with smiles, laughing about how fun it had been, how glad the girls were that the boys had driven over from Oxford. Smitty and Cole having to holler for Will, he and Mimi still sitting out on the dock making promises for the coming summer; Will saying that he'd come see her every weekend in Clarksdale. Mimi kissing him on the shoulder as she put her arms around his neck, whispering in his ear, "Be good and I'll see you soon." Will nodding, then turning and running along the wooden planks of the walk and across the yard and out to the road where Smitty and Cole sat with the truck already running and beers in hand. The driver seat empty.

"Aw, man, I can't drive," Will said, laughing. "No way I can stay on the road."

"C'mon," Smitty said, "It's the price you pay for scoring with Mimi Reston."

"Aw, man."

"C'mon," Smitty said, "You never drive. It's been your turn for four years."

"All right."

"I'll drive if you really can't," Cole said.

"Naw, I'm all right," Will said, "I'll get us home."

"That's my boy," said Smitty.

Pulling out on the road as the shadows of day's end stretched across the fields, the wind swirling in the truck, Smitty and Cole staring out at the land with squinted and focused eyes as if some final and collective answer might exist there, not even noticing at first as the truck moved off the pavement and into the shoulder gravel; Will realizing it and jerking the wheel back, the tires without hope on the loose gravel and the truck rolling out through the cotton field, no realization of time, only before and after. Smitty and Cole ending up on top of each other in the back seat of the truck, glass in their hair and across their arms, lines of blood on their skin.

"Smitty?"

"Cole?"

"I'm fine, where's Will?"

Crawling out of the broken back window, the dust from the field mixing with the blood on their hands, looking around in the half-light of dusk. No friend anywhere to be found. Then Cole reaching and taking hold of Smitty's arm, nodding towards the road where Will lay in the gravel flat on his stomach, one arm stretched out above his head as if reaching for something. These two boys running now toward the first tragedy of their lives, their panic so strangely incongruent to the calm, pastoral surroundings. Finding Will lifeless, blood matted in his hair and gravel caught in the glass scars on his back. Smitty simply lying down on top of Will, as if shielding him from some unseen force, sliding his arms up under Will's chest to hold him, then whimpering softly. Cole looking away, staring out across the lake with the dusk water so still, the enduring features of reality present as ever: a faint line of crimson sky lingering over the western tree line, year-around wood ducks circling in the air then lighting in the middle of the lake, the distant sound of laughter down on some stranger's dock.

Maria

Maria learned her first English at five, accidentally, hearing the strange words while walking past Anatole's garden. Anatole's wife, Becks, was originally from London, marrying Anatole during their years at voice school in Germany, initially coming to Kefalonia only to visit his family, then deciding she could never live anywhere else after laying eyes on such a place. Becks sang English hymns as she watered her vegetables, failing to notice the child Maria leaning against the fence, listening, head cocked to the side like a confused puppy. Maria stood silent for half an hour, the soft, foreign voice flowing over her like cold saltwater when she swam in the sea. After a while Becks caught Maria from the corner of her eye, approached her, extended a hand.

"Hello," she said.

"Yassus," Maria said, giving Becks her tiny palm.

"Yassu," Becks said, then again, "Hello."

"Ha-lo," Maria replied, questioning with her eyes. Becks nodded. "Hello."

"Hello," Maria said.

"Beautiful, you're a natural. I'll teach you English if you help me with my Greek."

Maria stood silent, watching this lady with her dirty blond hair and fair, faintly freckled skin. Becks pinched the material of

Maria's sundress in her fingers.

"Dress," she said, and nodded.

"Dress," Maria echoed.

"Glorious," Becks said, rustling Maria's hair. She walked over to a bush in the garden, pulled a Japanese plum from the branch. She held it up to Maria.

"Plum," Becks said. Maria giggled.

"Plum."

"Here," Becks said, handing the fruit to Maria. Maria took a bite.

"Plum," Maria repeated.

"Yes, my dear, plum."

Becks sent Maria home with her sweet prize, and that night, as her mother tucked her into bed, Maria grabbed the cloth of her mother's nightgown and said, "dress" — her mother dismissing the word as childish garble.

⌒

She learned quickly, often staying for supper, listening to Anatole and Becks talk about the day, repeating words she recognized, questioning them on words she didn't understand. When she started having entire English conversations with herself at home, Maria's father walked down to Anatole's house and offered to pay Becks for the generous instruction.

"She is my payment," Becks said in Greek, "She's a precious child."

"Yes," Maria's father said, "But all the time you give her, all the lessons."

Becks motioned Mr. Girgiou to the side as Maria played in the garden. She nodded her head towards Maria.

"Anatole and I," she said, "We are unable.... We can't have a Maria."

Mr. Girgiou nodded.

"The next time you and Anatole come to the café, do not bring any money."

"Oh Mr. Girgiou, we couldn't."

"You can and you will."

A year went by, then two. Maria's conversation became fluent. During the school year Maria met with Becks at night, learning to read Jack London's stories about wolves. She imagined these northern plains and mountains where packs of creatures ran through the moonlight, powdery snow rising at their feet. It was a dream to her, such places; beyond her to realize geography that didn't contain the sea. Becks insisted that these terrains were real, that they existed far away across the oceans. Maria's face would brighten with excitement, then go blank as her mind tried to grasp such images. She began to crave books, and Becks had to send away to England for more texts. She'd get caught reading novels in school, The Call of the Wild wedged inside her mathematics text during class. Her friends gave blank stares as she talked about Canadian men trying desperately to build fires in the snow.

Maria felt herself changing, her mind posing silent questions she couldn't ignore. As school years went by, she and Becks began discussing the books, their emphasis shifting from language to content, sometimes arguing over the author's purpose or certain themes.

"I've created a monster," Becks said once, shaking her head at this thirteen year old who'd already read more novels than most university graduates.

Maria's transformation, however, was completely internal. Her appearance to the island community remained normal. She continued working in the garden with her father and helping her mother cook and shell peas. She still swam in the sea for hours at a time, floating and spinning, her adaptation of flight.

Neither did she force her newfound language on her friends, rather hiding it from them best she could, especially as they entered high school. She didn't want to be considered different or even ambitious. She chatted with girlfriends about boys, jewelry. Flirted in class with boys she thought cute; held their hands when they'd all meet in Argostoli for a movie or just to walk the market street.

Inside, though, she was churning. Her world had become bigger, complicated. She knew now of distant people who lived life completely opposite from her, yet, seas and continents away, struggled with similar questions, similar fears. A sense of unification grew inside her, the longing to travel; to assemble this world inside her mind into concrete pictures her eyes could grasp. The woman in Steinbeck's Chrysanthemums tormented Maria for over a month, becoming the equivalent of a child's imaginary friend. She wanted conversation away from Kefalonia, with people possessing different ideas, so that she might test this emotional similarity which she saw in all the books. Near the end of secondary school a sense of entrapment attacked her, as if God's isolation of Kefalonia in the Ionian Sea had been aimed directly at her, binding her to the same life her parents and aunts and uncles had lived. Had they lived on the mainland, she might have considered running away. She was young, confused. When Becks found Maria crying in the garden one afternoon, Becks knew the tears didn't flow from a lost boyfriend, or adolescent insecurity, but rather from the knowledge of places, people, worlds unseen.

Becks organized it all before telling Maria. She even purchased the airfare.

"I have money, Maria," Becks told her, sitting in the garden as the shadow of the mountain spread over the sea at Katelios. "There's just not much to spend it on here in Kefalonia. It's one of the reasons I came here. But I wanted to do this, and I won't tolerate one word of dissent."

Maria began to smile as Becks continued.

"I've arranged a place for you to stay at the university in Durham. You'll have three interviews, two with an administrative committee and one with a few literature professors. You be yourself and show them all you know. There's no reason to hide your mind."

Maria's folks initially objected to the idea of Becks spending such money on their child, but when they saw their daughter's face, the hope in her eyes, they relented. One night, as they crawled in bed, Maria's mother began whimpering openly and softly to her husband.

"Things are different now," he said.

"I know."

The trip went as Becks assumed, Maria charming academia much the same way she'd charmed Becks as a child: Her hunger to learn shining through her attempted reserve, her previously earned knowledge breaking through the shield of humility she tried to maintain. The notification of scholarship allocation came only three weeks after she returned to the island. Maria ran down the dusty summer road to Becks' house where she and

Anatole sat drinking a glass of wine by the garden. Maria stopped by the fence, out of breath, raising the letter above her head in triumph. Becks broke out in true laughter before running to embrace her only student.

⌒

Two months of a Kefalonian summer separated her from the university at Durham. The days moved quickly, chatting with her father as he toiled in the garden, swimming in the early evenings off the rocks at Katelios, helping the young Yanni cook in the café. They unfolded similar to other summer days of her childhood, yet with a new precision. A clarity. As if her eyes developed a new perspective, able to grasp the depth of the landscape around her. Its history, its meaning. She knew her departure in the fall wouldn't be permanent, that she'd always return for holidays. Yet she was also aware of the internal changes surely to evolve as she studied on foreign soil, and she knew that this sort of partial metamorphosis would alter the way she viewed her homeland, both the land itself and its beliefs. So she took her time living these days, noticing what she hadn't noticed before, committing it to memory: a field of wildflowers on the road to Argostoli, the sailboats docked at Poros, the outline of Ithaki from the seaside cafés at Fiskardo. As if home would never look the same again.

One afternoon she attended a birthday party for her young

cousin, Thalia, in the village of Vlachata, on a patio that overlooked the sea. The tables were strewn with flowers and colored streamers. Two village men played the guitar and mandolin, taking requests from the children who danced at their feet. Maria sat in a circle of adults, yet neither listened nor contributed to the conversation. She was watching the children, the freedom in their steps. She wondered for a moment where it had all gone, these years of youth that had seemed endless along the way. At ten she never imagined being thirteen, at thirteen never sixteen, and so on, until now, eighteen and about to enter the larger world, she couldn't remember how it had passed so quickly, how she had become this young woman who drank wine with the adults and spoke a second language as naturally as her Greek. *We are much better as children. There are no strings to our laughter and our sleep is true and hard all through the night.*

After a while Thalia came and sat on Maria's lap. The resemblance between Maria and her little cousin proved striking. Folks laughed and shook their heads at the sight. Maria tapped her feet to the music and Thalia clapped her hands. They watched as the men brought out platters of goat meat and bowls of salad with tomatoes, cucumbers and onions. Thalia turned to her older cousin.

"Maria?" she asked.

"Yes?"

"Why do you want to leave us?"

Maria looked to the adults, as if her mother had put the child up to the question.

"It has nothing to do with wanting to leave," Maria said.

"Then why?"

"It's something only years can teach you. I can't say one sentence right now that would make you understand why I'm leaving Kefalonia."

"I don't understand," Thalia said. Maria shook her head, realizing the impossibility of explanation.

"Sometimes I don't understand it either," Maria said, "It's just something I have to do."

"You're scaring me," Thalia replied.

"Oh don't be scared. I'm going to be fine and the world will take care of me."

"Maria?"

"Yes?"

"Will you ever be able to come back to Kefalonia?"

"Of course. I can come back whenever I like."

"Will you come back for my birthday party next year?" Thalia asked.

"If you invite me."

"I invite you now to my birthday party next year."

"I accept," Maria said.

"Maria?"

"Yes?"

"Who will take me swimming in the sea at Katelios when you're gone?"

"You'll have to find somebody new."

"I don't like finding somebody new," Thalia said. Maria drew the child into her chest and kissed her forehead.

"I know," Maria said, "I imagine it's one of the hardest things we have to do."

"What?" Thalia said.

"Finding somebody new."

After the party Maria caught a ride back to Katelios. She went walking along the beach, tossing stones into the shallows, allowing the water to cool her bare feet. While relieved that she'd made the decision to explore another country, Maria was thankful for the month and a half before her actual departure. She felt suspended in this period of limbo, of transition, satisfied with the completion of the first fourth of her life, simply waiting to begin the second. As if life was allowing her a breather from itself, requiring only that she sleep and eat and pay attention to this land around her, this land of stone, mountain, sea — so that she be fully prepared when life returned her to the contest.

Maria started back to her parents' house, passing Becks' garden. She found her teacher and Anatole lounging on the patio. Maria stopped at the fence and greeted them in Greek.

"That's how it all started," Becks said.

"Yes," Maria said in English, "And it seems like only yesterday."

"Time is a cruel thing," Becks said, "Yesterday I was young and beautiful and singing in Germany." She motioned towards Anatole. "Then this Greek kid crosses my path and the next thing you know I'm a gardener in Kefalonia."

"I love your story," Maria said.

"We do too," Anatole said, "We just can't figure out how it got written so fast. The older we get, the quicker our pages turn."

"How was the birthday party?" Becks said.

"Lovely and sad. Little Thalia looks just like me. Watching her dance with her cousins made me want to be a child again."

"You still are a child," Anatole said.

"I wish, but we have your wife to thank for my transition into maturity."

"Wait a minute, I'm not taking all the blame for your impatience with youth. You were the one showing up at my house every night for a new book."

"Yes," Maria said, "But you knew about all the complications in those books. You knew they'd affect me."

"What was I to do? Deprive a child of the world?"

Maria grinned sarcastically. She bid them good-night and continued on to her parents' house, where she found her father sitting on the front steps, attempting to fix a rake that had broken apart from its wooden handle.

"Hello, my Maria," her father said.

"Hello, Anstice," she replied. She often called him by his first name when only acknowledging his presence. She sat down on the step and told him all about the birthday party.

"Why didn't you come?" she said.

"I suppose you've forgotten about the café that I run."

"Father, Yanni knows how to run the café. You don't always have to be looking over his shoulder."

"Yanni can only be in one place at one time. And I need him in the kitchen. Someone must charm the guests."

"That's it," Maria said. "You just like to sit out front and chat with the guests all day."

"Hospitality, my child. It is very important."

Several dogs passed on the road without purpose or care. Darkness settled over the island and the first star of night appeared in the half-lit sky. Maria wrapped her arms around her legs, bringing them in to her chest. Anstice set the rake down, unsatisfied. He breathed deeply and turned to his daughter.

"Are you all right?" he asked.

"Yes, just a little dreamy."

"Save them for your sleep," Anstice said. Then, after a long pause, "You know, if you change your mind about leaving, nobody will think less of you."

"Father, I'm going."

"I'm not trying to talk you out of it," he said, "I just want you to know that nobody is pressuring you to go. Even Becks would understand if you stayed."

Maria rustled his hair.

"You've never been very good at hiding your objectives, old man," Maria said. Anstice shrugged his shoulders. "But it's all right. Your motives are flattering."

She rose. As she entered the house she looked back to see her father returning to the rake. To his task.

That night, after reading a while, Maria lay in the clear darkness of her bedroom. Her eyes adjusted to the color of night. She could make out the objects adorning the room: a photograph of her father standing in front of his fishing boat, a framed print of an El Greco painting, the filled bookcase against the wall. *You adorn your nest with that which you love, objects and pictures of significance. But it all becomes part of the everyday until these personal icons don't move you anymore. Not because they lose their significance, but because you know they will be there, day in and day out. We are only moved by that which we can lose at a moment's notice, or by the sight of something we don't possess. Something that is not part of our everyday lives. All people want is greatness in their everyday life, so they frame prints of El Greco and place Joyce on their bookshelves and repeat Mozart on their stereos. Maybe we believe that these* aesthetics will somehow transfuse into our own blood and our lives will change into hours that possess the same drama as *Symphony No. 25 in G minor.* We cannot have such, though. Days are filled with the preparation of food. Cleaning. Tending to the plants. Often meaningless jabber between acquaintances. Trying to stay cool during the heat of day. These trivial, almost involuntary actions add up to a certain malaise that, if not offset by laughter or a solitary walk by the sea, can infect us to the point of wondering what it's all worth, if anything. And it's why we love the wine so, in hopes that the world might become a bit liquid instead of solid. Just enough that we forget its concrete, practical nature.

Outside her open window a slight breeze rose, rustling the olive trees, and to this sound young Maria slept in the same bedroom she'd slept all her short life.

She came up the steps of the café mid-morning and found Yanni preparing a bowl of salad for lunch. Maria poured herself a shot of coffee and watched her cousin.

"Did the sleep come again?" Yanni said.

"Yes, and it brought dreams this time."

"Of what?"

"Mama and Papa, of course," Maria answered.

"Sad?"

"Not necessarily," Maria said, "I dreamt of the summer before I left for England. How strange it was to simply live in wait of something to happen. Mama and Papa acted so funny that summer, as if I was leaving them forever." Yanni nodded his head without looking up. "I guess they were the ones," Maria said.

"What?"

"They were the ones that left me forever."

"Stop it," Yanni said.

"I'm strong now, Yanni, I feel comfortable talking about it."

"There's no reason to test yourself."

"I'll say what I like, thank you," Maria said.

"Sometimes I think you're harder on me than your father was."

"Oh please, Yanni. Remember how Papa used to cuss you for slicing the tomatoes too wide."

"My uncle was a kind man," Yanni said.

"Quit being so proper. They're gone. You can say what you like now."

"Please Maria."

"If you can't speak honestly about the dead, who can you speak honestly about?"

"This conversation is over," Yanni said, placing the salad into the cooler.

Maria walked out and sat on the steps of the café, sipping her coffee. She looked out over the sea, the same white sun climbing the eastern sky, Zachynthos resting an unknown distance away on the horizon. *So this will be my life.*

She finished her coffee, set the empty mug on a table, started down the street. Stray dogs approached her and she patted their heads without stopping. Several followed at her heels in seeming obedience, as if believing she could lead them to a place of significance.

She found Becks on the back patio, reading. Her old instructor, now with streaks of grey adorning the hair around her ears. Faint lines of age traversing the skin under her eyes.

"Professor Becks," Maria said.

Becks rose and opened the gate. They stared at each other a moment with looks of bittersweet expression, as if some truth long since hinted at had been confirmed. They embraced, Becks whispering, "Are you making it?"

"Quite," Maria said, managing a weak grin as they released each other. Becks took her hand and led her to the patio.

"What are you reading?" Maria said.

"A gardening book. Instructional."

"Becks, please, a gardening book?"

"What? You think literature is hard on the young, you should see what it can do to the old. Instructional books are much easier on the heart."

Maria looked around the garden as if she'd been absent a good long while, checking to see what had changed, what had grown. Becks watched her.

"What is it?"

"Nothing. Well, I don't know, it's difficult to explain."

"Try," Becks said.

"Okay, when do you get satisfied with all of this?" Maria motioned towards the setting around them.

"With all of what?"

"With this. With what your eyes see. What morning did you walk out and say, 'Okay, this was the same garden as yesterday in the same place as yesterday and all will be the same tomorrow and I am happy knowing that it will all be the same for the rest of my life?'"

"Goodness, you are more troubled than I thought." They laughed and Becks touched the inside of Maria's arm. "I am teasing," Becks said, "I know exactly what you're talking about."

"You do?"

"Yes, you believe that the grass is greener on the other side."

"Oh please."

"Seriously, it's exactly what you're talking about," Becks said, "You just don't like to hear it in those terms because, put that way, it doesn't sound very dramatic or complicated. But that's all it is. You're asking me when I quit coveting other lives or situations that I thought existed."

"I think you're putting words in my mouth."

"No, I'm just getting to the heart of the matter. What's troubling you is that you still wake up and wonder if you're really supposed to be in another place, doing something else, spending time with other people, living a different life." Maria looked down at her lap. "See, I've hit a nerve. Maria, I spent over a decade as your teacher. You don't think I learned to read your emotions over that time?"

"Okay, so maybe I wear my heart on my sleeve a little more than I'd like to believe."

"It's not a fault, only a trait."

"So what's the answer?"

"Well, you can imagine that there's no concrete answer. But I will say two things. The only day you can live is the one given to you, and two, someone will always seem to be living a more dramatic, fulfilled life than you. Always. No matter who you are."

"That's comforting."

"It's not meant to be comforting, it's meant to be true."

"I know. I'm just struggling."

Becks placed her hand on top of Maria's. "Maria, you've just lost your parents. You have every reason to struggle."

"Damn the books," Maria said.

"Don't damn the books," Becks said, "You're reaching for something that doesn't exist and your recent loss simply makes it hurt more."

"Listen to you, from English teacher to psychologist."

"Well, I have to vent my ambitions somehow. Given that Anatole sentenced me to the eternal role of gardener."

"I had better get back to the café. I let Yanni do most of the work as it is."

"Just live the day the best you can," Becks said, "And try to enjoy the simple things, if only the wind coming off Ainos."

"Now you're getting dramatic."

"I'd rather say pretty words than practical ones."

"And I'd rather hear them."

Maria walked slowly back to the café, kicking stones along the partially paved street. She thought of Keane again, how she missed their walks along the river Weir at Durham. How they'd stop and sit on a stretch of fresh grass, a low mist hanging above the water. Watching the crew teams oar past with their graceful, silent rhythms.

Cole

He watched the concrete sprawl of the city change into low pine hills. Small farms of row crop dissected by creeks that ran clearer as they reached the first mountains of Carolina. They ascended into a blinding sheet of white cloud, and he drew the plastic cover over the window.

It's now that you actually consider what you're doing. On a plane with strangers, most going to places where they do not speak the language, where they do not know the people. I guess I'm one of them now, although not totally of my own accord. I just didn't feel like fighting Mama about this one. It always bothered her that I hadn't traveled, hadn't seen the land and people on the other side of the sea. So here I am, when I should be fishing that crappie lake in Tupelo with Smitty. Or country road riding with that Kara girl. She kissed me lovely last night.

Maybe it's a flaw, my homeliness, only wanting to be amidst cotton fields and hardwood bottoms. Maybe I should want to see other places, other lives. I've just never had the desire. My life and the land surrounding seemed to fill my cup. I never saw any point in trying to live an existence that wasn't dealt to me. Sometimes my folks act unsatisfied with the south, as if they stay in Memphis simply out of respect to their roots, or more specifically, to the land Father inherited. They have the money to live anywhere they want, but they don't leave because they know where the money came from. It came from Delta fields that produced cotton tall as a man stood.

I don't know why cane thickets and cypress swamps and kudzu stands along the highway strike me as beautiful. Most people would consider them eyesores. I find them picturesque. One of my English professors in prep school corrected me, said that mountains and seas were picturesque, that Mississippi was simply authentic. I told him that Mississippi was picturesque to me and he responded that picturesque wasn't a term that I could simply bend for my own use. I told him to go to hell. Mama got a little upset over that one.

Cole rubbed his eyes and opened an outdoor magazine he'd brought. He'd been thinking of Smitty all day, how upset he'd gotten the night before, all those tears out of nowhere. It's going to be harder for Smitty, because he can't let go of those things he said before we left Moon Lake. But those words meant nothing; we say things like that every day. Only tragedy brings significance to our conversations.

Cole read an article on mid-summer bass. How to catch lunkers in ninety-plus heat. It didn't contain anything he didn't already know, but it was well written, and Cole always loved to read these articles if only to remind himself that folks existed out there who loved fishing as much as he. It's all about that moment of complete presence when a fish strikes, that moment where there is no world anymore, no time, no girls that you once loved who are gone, no *parents wanting you to do new things, no hardships, no struggles; only that you are alive and the fish is alive, and for a brief moment a seeming immortality becomes suspended in the taut, stretched line, you and the fish fighting to capture it, yet it disappearing the moment the fish escapes, as if it wasn't ever there. Maybe it was only a figment, a hope. Yet fishermen return again and again trying to capture it, losing themselves in the intimacy of the struggle. A return. To oxbow lakes and river eddies. Streams. Even the sea. Yes, the sea, although I know nothing about the sea. But I imagine it's still the same.*

Around the plane people moved about, chatting to folks in the rows behind them. Cole thought about the solitude of the trip, how strange it was for a Mississippi boy to travel to Greece alone. To stay with a family he'd never met. Cole's parents had sat him down briefly, a week after Will's funeral, and reminded him about their special friends in Kefalonia. How for some odd reason, even with the language barrier, they'd become friends with the Kappatoses on their honeymoon so many years ago. His father told him that Mr. Kappatos was a considerable landowner there on the island, even though it was nothing like the plantation farmland Cole was used to. Mr. Kappatos spoke a bit of broken English, and he and Cole's father somehow got on the subject of land investing at the small café in Katelios and began a relationship both friendly and professional. *Money was somehow always involved with Father's friends, although you wouldn't ever know it. He drives an old Scout to this day.*

Cole's father had explained the several land deals he'd bargained over the years with Mr. Kappatos, how lucrative they'd been because of the dollar's power in Kefalonia. His father spoke of what caring people the Kappatoses were, that they would welcome Cole into their home if the boy wanted to come. Cole had listened half-heartedly, Will still fresh on his mind. His attention span had all but disappeared since that afternoon on Moon Lake, and he simply nodded when his mother actually said that they thought it would be good for him to get away for a little while.

"I'll go," Cole had mumbled.

"Well, Son," his mother said, "It's a significant trip. Should you think about it more?"

"Would y'all be suggesting if you didn't want me to go?"

She had looked to his father, as if asking for help.

"We just think a trip might help, considering what's happened. Maybe it will take your mind off things."

"Nothing will," Cole said, "But I'll go. I said I'll go."

He immediately left the room, not allowing his parents to go on. They'd grown apart in the years since Cole left for Oxford, not necessarily out of conflict but merely out of absence. Cole never came home save Christmas and Thanksgiving, choosing to spend his vacations at the hunting camp, or going home with

friends from down in the Delta to see new woods, new fields. His
personality, in a way, seemed contradictory. He loved to travel,
but only inside the borders of his Mississippi, on potholed highways
and gravel roads, racing to another duck hole or some deer woods
his buddies hadn't hunted in a few years, ten thousand conversations
in the still blackness of his truck, driving in the dawn with
friends, often Will himself, drinking coffee, bullshitting about
how to call flight ducks or how far away a deer can really smell
you. Other friends from Memphis invited him on ski trips to
Colorado, summer beach trips to the Gulf Coast; but he always
passed, making up some excuse of prior plans. And he would
always have prior plans, but they never extended beyond crappie
fishing with jigs at North Lake, or shooting skeet out at Sardis,
or camping in the Yocona River bottom with mosquitoes that
Smitty used to say could stand flat-footed and screw a duck.
Hardly dates that people would consider unbreakable in comparison
to the white sand beaches of Florida. Yet for Cole, he wouldn't
miss them for the world. His favorite of all places remained
the sandbar at Moon Lake, watching an August sun fall below the
river levee.

Yet he relented this time, for his mother's sake, and maybe
somewhere in his troubled mind Cole agreed with his folks.
There had been no other experience in his short life that brought
such tragedy, such perspective. His second cousin, Laney, had

died of leukemia at fourteen, but she'd had it for a long time and the expectation of her death seemed to ease the intensity of its bite. And the passing of his grandfather had arrived when it was supposed to arrive, after seventy five years of life. Will's accident was a sudden, piercing jolt of reality that broke down all constructions Cole had formulated of the world around him. Will embodied youth and innocence, always living on the threshold of danger yet never appearing to realize it, like a lost retriever sniffing around on a highway shoulder.

Cole remembered the time when he and Will and Smitty were duck hunting a rice field in Tallahatchie County. They'd been drinking beer in the blind for several hours, and Will, fidgeting with the safety on his double barrel shotgun, accidentally discharged it. He'd been holding the gun upright as he stood against the front of the blind, talking about what he'd like to do to some girl from Texas in his history class. After the roar of the shot, they all decided that the spread of pellets must have missed his chin by less than an inch.

"I guess that was a warning," Will had said.

"For what?" Smitty asked.

"Good Lord didn't want me talking about Texas girls like that."

Cole napped for an hour, and then retrieved his journal out of his backpack. He wrote about Lily, her subtle features, how her hair would tickle his nose when he slept in the crook of her body. He wrote about her soft, thin hands, the way she'd rub her nails across the inside of his forearm, or through the back of his hair as they drove through the Mississippi afternoon to Sardis Lake. They loved to ride with each other, no matter the destination, simply to watch the land pass before them. Through old hardwood bottoms, over pine hills. Past endless Delta fields. Something about witnessing the southern terrain with Lily drew him to her. Some sort of inherent ritual that possessed his heart.

They met on the porch of the Grocery. A still August evening. The sun beginning its descent, hanging low on the brim of a southern sky. Shadows cast across the courthouse lawn as Cole and Will and Smitty drank whisky and waters on the overhanging porch, watching as folks ambled past on the sidewalk beneath them. Cars drifted around the Square, seemingly slowed by the heat. Cole was telling the boys about a dove field he'd planted in sunflowers up on his father's horse farm in west Tennessee when Lily and Katherine Hancock stepped out on the porch. They took the table next to the boys, sipping their drinks slowly, whispering about something the boys couldn't hear. Cole continued on about the dove field, and after another round of Maker's, Smitty dismissed himself early on the grounds of a dawn fishing trip to Sardis. Will wasted no time.

"Y'all sit with us," he said. Katherine and Lily looked at each other. "C'mon," Will said, "It's what we all want." They laughed and Cole shook his head at Will's unrivaled social courage. The girls pulled their chairs up to the table, and it began.

If memory only allowed one evening from my year with Lily, I would have to choose that first night. That dusk. Watching Lily react so graciously to Will's eloquent, whisky-induced mediation of the conversation; listening to her brief, relevant additions to the dialogue. For an hour I couldn't tell who Will was targeting, Lily or Katherine; yet there was no indecision for me. At one point Lily had gone to the restroom while Katherine welcomed new friends arriving on the porch. I leaned across the table and, with all the seriousness that I could muster, whispered these words to Will: "Lily. Please."

Of course only Lily's answer mattered. And I received it, later that night, sitting on Smitty's tailgate in the driveway of our house off 9th Street. We'd walked home from the Square through the warm Mississippi night, the streetlights humming, Lily offering me generous laughs as I rambled on about times spent with Will and Smitty and other boys who cared for fish and woods and fields. I kissed her. Lightly, quickly. Immediately looking for an invitation to return. Some recognizable signal that meant again, please, do it again, this time for a good long while. She took my hand and led me across the yard, complaining that the mosquitoes were eating her alive as we walked up the front steps. Just inside the door she pressed me gently against the wall and touched my bottom lip with her finger. Strangely she embraced me for a good minute or two before returning the kiss.

I slept on the couch, Lily in my room — it being the first night and all she said. I stared at the ceiling and imagined her bare back, how it would feel to press my face against it. Lying there, I never again wanted to share a roof with Lily and not be curled beside her.

The following weeks brought a relatively routine process: lunches at the soul food place on the Pontotoc highway; Thursday night trips to Taylor for catfish; Saturday afternoons perched on the porch at the Grocery with a circle of others. Though Smitty said little about my newfound companionship, I could tell he accepted its reality. He genuinely liked Lily, though they never became close. Smitty only became attached to certain crappie poles and dedicated retrievers. Will, on the other hand, drew constant happiness from the sight of Lily and I together, often claiming responsibility for the union.

One cool night in late October, tailgating in the Grove after a football game, Lily asked if we could turn it in early. We said our goodbyes, then walked back to the house through town in near silence. I wondered if something was wrong. A block before the house she took my hand. I followed her to my room and waited for an explanation. Something I had said earlier, something I had done. Instead she undressed me and we made love for the first time. And again just after midnight.

Night somewhere over the sea. Lights turned out in the cabin, folks sleeping. Cole sat awake with a Field & Stream in his lap, attempting to read.

He didn't know how long they'd been in the air, or how many hours left until they landed in Athens. *To be honest, I don't really care. It would be fine with me if we just stayed up here for good, never arriving at a destination. That way we wouldn't ever be disappointed with how a place turns out as opposed to our ignorant expectations. What are you saying? You don't even know what the hell you're saying. You ought to just quit all the thinking and read your magazine, learn what lures are best in lily pads in mid-summer and which ones are best in deep water. Then your mind can be filled with concrete, useful knowledge and not these unanswerable thoughts about how this life is supposed to turn out. Life turns out in one way, and that's years and months and days and moments. Whatever content unfolds within these measures of time is irrelevant. You simply live a succession of days until they add up into a life and then you bid your farewell. It's not so damn complicated. Just try and do as much fishing as you can and you'll be all right.*

He wondered if Mr. and Mrs. Kappatos knew of his loss, if his folks had disclosed the nature of the trip. *I'm sure they did. I hope they don't try and counsel me, try to force an atmosphere of healing upon me. I doubt it. I'll probably have enough trouble just trying to communicate with them. But that's all right, the shallower the conversation the better. What's so strange is knowing that the coming two weeks will be the only time you ever spend with these folks. I guess there's nothing wrong with temporary friendship. You probably care more for the girl back at the barbecue place in New Albany than some folks you've known all your life. She was a looker, no doubt. May have to swing back through on the return trip. Feels kind of strange to be looking again, Lily being gone and all. Part of me wants to know what Lily's doing, part of me doesn't. Too much risk in finding out. Sure, if you find out she's been thinking about you, then all is well. But if it turns out some Yankee cat has her spinning again, then some sleepless nights will await. And there's nothing worse than being awake when the rest of the world is sound asleep. No lonely like that. Well maybe, but let's not go there.*

Cole retrieved an incomplete manuscript from his backpack. It was a hunting story about a boy who'd gotten separated from his father while hunting mallards in flooded bottomland timber. The boy was chasing a crippled drake through the backwater, the duck diving every time the boy got close, resurfacing, diving again. By the time he was able to shoot the cripple he'd walked a quarter mile through the woods. Looking around, the terrain in every direction lay the same: cypress knees, big oaks, patches of smartweed. The boy couldn't remember which way he'd come.

Heavy cloud cover hid any help from the sun. So he guessed, trudging in his waders through the thigh-deep floodwater, walking for half an hour before accepting that he'd chosen wrong and was headed deeper into the bottom. He called for his father, then listened. Nothing. He called again. Again. Then screaming loudly as possible, the sound echoing through the flooded woods like the boom of his double barrel. Nothing. The boy leaned against a tree, exhausted from hollering. Then he heard it. The sharp cranking of the old 15 horse motor, his father revving it a moment, backing it off, putting it in gear. He prayed for the sound to become louder, nearer, for the sight of his father and lab retriever to come meandering through the woods in the johnboat. But the hum of the old motor lessened, faded to silence.

The boy dropped his chin to his chest. He knew his father would search all night for him if need be, but even that didn't encourage him. You could search for days in this bottom and not cover a fourth of it. Or cover the same square mile over and over again, thinking you're somewhere else. It's a maze down here, the boy in the story thought, and it looks like I need to find a ridge to spend the night on. Build a fire.

That's all Cole had written. He couldn't decide whether to let the boy freeze or to let him be a good scout, surviving in the winter woods until help finally came. Cole knew the truth, but didn't know if he could go through with it. He was tired of writing tragedy, but he didn't know how to write anything else. In a way, prior to Will's death, he had written tragic stories to punish himself, to try and create some sadness in a life that had unfolded rather pleasantly. Cole often felt guilty for the happiness of his youth, writing of sadness in an attempt to somehow experience it. But now, with Will gone, he wished that he'd never written despair into his stories, often cursing himself for being so ungrateful before.

He stared at the white space where the words had temporarily ended. He shook his pen and began, allowing the things he knew about boys and woods to fill his thoughts, translating it onto the page the only way he knew how: raw and blatant, like the heat from a wood stove. Although he tried to fight against it, the words of the story moved toward the boy's death. Cole stopped, closed his eyes. He so wanted the boy to live, to be able to hunt with his father again. He pictured the timeline of the boy's life. A girl maybe. Sunday afternoon rides through the country. He wanted the boy to someday teach his grandson how to call ducks, but he knew there was only one way to finish the story. So Cole did not finish it. He folded the manuscript and placed it in the seat pouch between a contemporary magazine and the instruction booklet for emergency evacuations.

He woke as they broke out of the clouds. Cole raised the window cover: red mountains littered with shadows. Villages at the bottom of sunlit valleys, like some painting he'd once seen of a land far away. They were flying along the coast, and he glanced down at the sea, light surf breaking against the rocks of shore.

After a few moments Athens appeared in the distance, built between a line of mountains and the sea. White stone buildings, red roofing. *Pretty close to what I imagined, except now it's true. Now I believe it.*

They exited the plane just off the runway, walking the short distance over to the terminal, warm wind blowing down off the mountains, piercings of sunlight streaming down through the scattered afternoon cloud cover. In the terminal Cole listened to the language, allowed the foreign sounds to wash over him, ignoring comprehension, only hearing voices and not words. *It's nice to be the stranger for once. To have an excuse to know nothing.*

He fetched his baggage, then sat down on a bench. A stray dog wandered in through the sliding doors, walked over and lay down at Cole's feet, as if he'd found his lost owner. The front of the terminal was glass and Cole stared out at the city, thinking how he could simply catch a cab and get lost in this place, this country. To truly disappear, without telling anyone. *This is how people start from scratch. They disappear. You could do it you know, especially here, with your coal black hair and thick eyebrows, your olive skin. You could start over if you wanted to. But there's no reason to, bud, there's no reason to fix what's not broken. Remember, nothing happened to you, something happened to Will. Don't be claiming other people's tragedies so you can feel sorry for yourself. Now go catch the puddle jumper.*

In an hour Cole was airborne again. He listened to the loud humming of twin props, watched the sea pass under him, the reflections of sunlight off the clear water almost blinding. After a few minutes he started noticing islands dotting the landscape, as if a great flood had arrived on a land of mountains, all the people building their lives on each summit, hoping the water wouldn't rise any more. They became many, and he could see distant islands resting on the farthest horizon of sea, the edge of the world. He imagined having his own boat and visiting each one, fishing every coast of every island.

For the first time he considered the possibility that his mother knew what she was doing. Sending him here and all.

⤢

The Kappatoses waited on the terrace of the small airport at Kefalonia. There had been only ten or twelve people on the plane, and the American boy Cole Morgan was obvious as he exited the plane in his dark blue jeans and button-down, khaki shirt. Mr. Kappatos looked to his wife and smiled.

"Cole," Mr. Kappatos said as the boy made his way up the ramp.

"Hello," Cole said, gripping Mr. Kappatos' hand, then hugging Mrs. Kappatos slightly with his arm.

"It's beautiful here," Cole said. Mr. Kappatos cocked his head, stood silent. "The island is beautiful," he repeated. "Kefalonia, beautiful."

"Yes, yes," Mrs. Kappatos said, taking her husband's hand, then Cole's in her free one, "Thank you much. You see more now."

The road to Katelios wound along the southern plateau of the island, the sea visible and endless to the south, the interior mountain Ainos daunting and steep to the north. Small vineyards dotted the fields between the road and coast, rows of olive trees and grapes. Goats grazed in herds amidst the rocky sagegrass terrain. They drove through a village every couple of miles or so where old, dark-skinned men sat on benches in front of cafés, children playing on the sidewalk.

The language barrier lessened the burden of conversation, and Cole rode with a confident ease knowing that the Kappatoses didn't expect him to try and make small talk. The windows were down to his approval, warm wind flushing his face as he scanned the landscape, the blue sea like a magnet to his eyes. *Even a river rat can appreciate the sight of that son of a bitch. It's almost too much to look at.*

"Farm," Mr. Kappatos said, pointing towards about an acre of olives and grapes.

"Right there, that little garden," Cole said, looking.

Mr. Kappatos shrugged his shoulders in confusion, and Cole remembered he wasn't talking to Smitty.

"Yes, farm," he said.

It was late afternoon, the light crisp. They descended the last hill into the valley at Katelios, turning onto the Kappatoses' graveled drive, their house set back on several acres of grassland and in the shade of a few trees. Just down the road lay the main street with its cafés and flats to rent, newspaper stands. Off to the side of the house was a small garden with tomatoes and peas and squash and watermelon. Cole shook his head. *This is right up my alley, there's just no woods and the water's got salt in it. But it's country all right, and quiet. I ought to have more faith in Mama.*

They ate bread and tomatoes and a meat pie Mrs. Kappatos had cooked earlier in the day. Cole hadn't eaten much on the flight, and the warm, spicy food lifted his spirits. He tore a piece of bread from the loaf, dipped it in a saucer of olive oil and held it aloft.

"Delicious," he said to Mrs. Kappatos, motioning to his plate with the bread.

"Good, good," she said, "I knew you hungry."

When they finished eating Mr. Kappatos led Cole outside to the garden. He pointed to the rows, explaining in his best possible English what grew, when he had planted, when each vegetable would be ripe. Cole nodded, trying to pay attention, his eyes distracted by the sea and the outline of a great island in the distance.

"Zachynthos," Mr. Kappatos said.

"What?"

"Zachynthos. I see you look." Mr. Kappatos pointed across the sea.

"How far?" Cole said.

Mr. Kappatos shrugged his shoulders. "No swim there," he said.

They walked behind the house where two acres of grape bushes lay in rows. Mr. Kappatos spoke of September, when all his nieces and nephews would come and help him pick the grapes, laughing, shouting at each other, racing to see who could pick the most the fastest. Then he led Cole to the basement, showing him the large brick tub where they dumped the grapes. Cole followed the man's broken English rather well, appreciating how much information was relayed with so few words. *It's always best to* reduce ourselves to the simplest of terms. People are the source of their own confusion. They try to justify and articulate and excuse all their sincerest emotions when the only words necessary are I hurt, I love, I long. Lily and I said too many things to each other those last weeks of school before she left. All those nights of debating our emotions should have been spent recounting the year we shared. Inside we believed our forking of roads should have held some sort of intense significance, and arguing dramatically seemed the best way to bring about such significance. Yet just as Mr. Kappatos explains his life with deliberate terms, I should have looked at Lily and only said: I hurt, I love, I long. We thought our lives so complex, so intricate, our emotions in more turmoil than anyone could understand. Yet it was all rather basic, looking back. A decision had been made. Lily would leave in May, I would stay. We lacked the courage, or confidence, to make any sort of commitment, and in our incompetence we both felt the need to justify all the reasons for embarking on separate journeys. We acted as if some inherent promise had been broken, when actually there had been no promise at all. This life only intersects two paths; it doesn't turn them in the same direction. That's up to us. How often we excuse our lack of courage with, "It wasn't meant to be." I may be the greatest culprit of such offense.

Mr. Kappatos pointed to the barrels of wine sitting against the wall. Some of the barrels were over twenty years old, he told Cole, then took a cup from the shelf and drew a small taste of the oldest wine. He handed the cup to Cole. Cole sniffed it, then sipped. His face drew up as if he'd sucked a lemon.

"It's like shooting whisky," Cole said. Mr. Kappatos laughed.

"The old, the more..." Mr. Kappatos said, punching the air to explain the intensity he couldn't formulate with English.

They went upstairs and found Mrs. Kappatos finishing the dishes. She put her hand on Cole's shoulder and told him that he was welcome to everything, that he didn't have to ask when hungry, that he could help himself to all the food and wine he wanted. Cole nodded in appreciation, and Mr. Kappatos took him out to the small guest house by the garden where he'd be staying. Inside sat a bed, a chair, a desk. On the wall hung an oil painting of Mary, a white light shining down out of the clouds upon her face. On the desk, a vase of flowers. The lone window open, an afternoon breeze fluttering the floor length curtains.

"You need," Mr. Kappatos said, "You come to house. You get anything."

"Appreciate it," Cole said.

"Now I sleep," the old man said, "This time all days. Sleep this time all days."

Cole looked at his watch. Late afternoon. He remembered Mama talking about all the glorious naps she took in Kefalonia.

"Siesta," Mr. Kappatos said, "Sleep time. You go. You walk wherever. No matter to us."

"Thanks."

"Jeep," Mr. Kappatos said. He pointed out the door. Cole had noticed the jeep when they pulled up. The old man handed him the keys. "You drive if want. Be safe."

"Yessir."

"Now I sleep." He patted Cole on the shoulder and walked back to the house.

Cole lay down on the bed, placed his hand on his full stomach. He thought about Will, then Smitty. His boys from Mississippi. *One gone, the other not doing so fine. You're not doing so fine yourself, old boy, so don't start with the sympathy; although Smitty will be doing a lot worse when the dog days of summer set in and the fish quit biting. That's always been the hardest part of the year for Smitty: no fish biting, nothing in season to hunt. Simply waiting for fall's return.*

Fall always resembled a promise of sorts, of cooler days and wind in the evenings, a return of those absent during the summer, the arrival of new faces. We always frequented the bars late August, early September, to see all the pretty faces from places like Clarksdale and Greenwood and Meridian, Tupelo and Columbus, Leland and Yazoo City. It was your way in, your trump card, to know someone from these places. All you had to do was ask the girl where she was from, and when she responded you simply said, "Oh, so you know...," and she would laugh and say of course she does. Then it would all be easy, and

you would begin to tell stories about your common friends from common
places, because you wanted to keep it all going, the high, the spirit of
beginnings, of fall in Mississippi. It made you feel alive again after the
sluggish end of summer, to be laughing with a strange girl. Although
she was never really strange, for in a way you already knew her.

In a way you already knew them all.

So you won't say strange but at least new, and laughing with a new
girl with her brown shoulders and slow drawl and the whisky going
down like candy until your face got all flushed and hot, you thought:
this was life. And to look across the bar and see Smitty and Will doing
the same thing reassured you that all would be well forever. Watching
Smitty court a strange girl with a tumbler of Maker's in hand may be
as fine a sight as the sun going down over the river levee at Moon
Lake. It made you give thanks to the fall, for offering Smitty that kind
of courage. But don't forget about the Maker's, she's been known to
dole out a bit of courage herself.

Now sleeping, this boy Cole Morgan, in Kefalonia, in the village of Katelios, the long journey and good meal catching up with
him, carrying him deep into rest. Dreaming scattered images,
faces, voices. Will, Smitty, Lily. His mother when he was a child.
For awhile he lost the dream, only sleep, true rest without the
interrupting mind. Just before he woke he saw Lily on the front
stoop of his porch. She said, "I was wrong to leave Mississippi,
Cole. I'll never leave again."

He rose and felt the wind through the window. The land now in the shadow of the mountain but the last shine of day still painting the sea. He rubbed his eyes and put on his boots and started across the small, stony pasture with its wildflowers and sagegrass. Made his way around the edge of the village and walked out upon the beach. A light stench of seaweed lay on the rocks, salt clinging to the air. Downbeach he could see a man anchoring a small fishing boat to the shallows and beyond that the southern tip of Kefalonia stretching far out into the sea like an arrow.

Maria

She worked through siesta, cleaning the floor beneath the tables and dusting the pictures on the wall. She softly sang the old songs of Kefalonia just loud enough for Yanni to hear as he began his cooking preparations for the evening specials. She knew that Yanni loved to hear her sing, even though he never expressed any compliment. When finished with her tasks, Maria called to him: "I'm going for a walk before the guests start to show."

"All right, please be brief. It will be very difficult for me to host the guests and cook for them at the same time. I do not think they want to sit in the kitchen."

"I'll be back shortly," she said, amused when Yanni attempted sarcasm in English.

On the beach she knelt and rubbed a stray dog. It rolled over and exposed its belly. Maria talked to it as she scratched, telling the stray what a glorious, wandering life it possessed, eating scraps from the cafés and sleeping on the beach under the stars with the breeze coming in off the sea. She walked on, watching the sunlight sparkle on the ripples of water, gulls circling and soaring in the slight wind without effort, Zachynthos standing true and persistent in the distance.

She looked downbeach and saw him, a young man staring out at the sea as if waiting for an arriving journeyman. She paused, then walked on. He kept his attention on some unknown point on the horizon, but she knew he'd noticed her. She tried to remember if she'd been singing as she walked, blushing slightly in the possibility.

"Yassu," she said. The boy turned.

"Hello," he said. Maria froze.

"You're not Greek," she said.

"Not that I know of."

"Are you lost?"

"Kind of," Cole said, "But I've got a place to stay so I'm not real worried about it." Maria cocked her head in slight confusion.

"I know who you are."

"You do?" Cole said.

"You're the new guest of my godparents, the American boy."

"I didn't know they had spread the word," he responded.

"They only said something to me because they thought you'd enjoy a little English language while you were here."

"And you're the only one in the village who speaks it?"

"The only one our age."

"So how old are you?"

"Twenty-three going on forty," Maria answered. "And you?"

"Twenty-two wishing for eighteen."

"Why?"

"I miss ignorance," Cole said.

"Then you're claiming wisdom?"

"I've got enough figured out to know I don't want to figure any more."

"Are all Americans so open with their thoughts?"

"Only southerners."

"Why?"

"Because the south still believes in drama."

"I'll agree with that," Maria said, "They say it's why they started the Civil War. They loved their drama too much."

"A Civil War expert in Greece. I'll be damned."

"I took some American history classes," Maria said.

"Why?"

"I've always been curious about places I've never been."

"I wouldn't have thought that Greek schools offered United States history," Cole said.

"I studied in England," she said, "Where again are you from?"

"Mississippi. Oxford, Mississippi."

"Faulkner," Maria said.

"Yeah," Cole said, skipping a rock across the shallows, "And my parents live in Memphis. Know anyone from there?"

"Elvis."

"And Europeans make fun of American tourists," Cole said,

"Y'all are twice as bad as we are."

"I know more about Faulkner than where he's from," Maria said as she sat down on a flat rock next to Cole.

"So do a lot of people."

"I thought American southerners were known for their friendly kindness."

"I'm just playing with you," he said. "I'm grouchy from my nap. We don't take afternoons off in the States."

"Well, you should. It's natural to sleep in the heat of the day."

"You're right," he agreed. "So you're a Faulkner and United States history expert. You must be quite valuable at dinner parties."

"Not in Kefalonia," Maria said, "Most folks in Kefalonia aren't concerned with such subjects." Cole nodded. Maria watched him. "This is strange," she said.

"What is?"

"Talking this casually and openly with someone I've just met. It's not a very Greek thing to do."

"Well."

"I guess my folks would have expected me to be more reserved with a strange boy, more careful. I don't know. Hey, wait. I don't even know your name."

"Cole. Cole Morgan."

"Maria. Maria Girgiou."

Cole offered his hand. He watched hers rise.

"Listen," she said, "I've got to go serve supper."

"To whom?"

"My guests." Cole watched her, his eyes needing more explanation. "I run a café down the street," she said. Cole laughed. "What?" she said.

He hesitated a moment and then added, "I've got a thing for café girls."

"I'm confused," Maria said.

"You should be. I'm confused too. I think we all are."

"Let's talk before your nap next time. Sleep makes you too complex."

"There's going to be a next time?" Cole said.

"If you'd like," she said. "I'm not too proud to admit that it's nice having someone my age around. Everyone here seems to be ten or eighty." Maria scratched her ankle, tucked her black hair behind her ears. "Why don't you come down to the café after breakfast tomorrow? Mid-morning. We'll go play. I'll show you some places."

"Mr. Kappatos said I could use the jeep if I wanted."

"Bring it," Maria said. "Bye, Cole Morgan."

"Take care," he said.

She ascended the steps of the café in full smile, greeting one couple she knew who'd been in the village all week, then a family of newcomers, asking forgiveness for her tardiness, bringing out dishes of tzaziki and loafs of fresh bread on the house, bragging about the synagrida Yanni had prepared for tonight, how it had always been her favorite. Yanni watched her, confused at the brilliance of her mood.

All night she sat with the guests, much like her father used to, asking them about their families and homes, her sincere interest making the guests feel special, unique, proud of wherever in the world they hailed from. Maria's mood infiltrated the entire dining room, and folks asked for more flasks of wine, more bread, the volume of chatter growing louder and friendlier as the night drifted on. The sea became dark with the half-moonlight flickering across the water and the lights of Zachynthos hanging low in the distant darkness, as if the entire scene had been conjured or painted or written about, but not actually lived. Yet they were all living it, and Maria in the midst of them, floating, even pouring herself a few glasses of wine, which was normally against the rules. But what were rules during a life that you only get to live for a little while. "This is no dress rehearsal," Keane had told her one night next to the river Weir, "We only get one run-through."

Folks conversed with those at other tables, shared their wine carafes with strangers. At one point around ten, an old man from Florence stood up in the seat of his chair, his wine glass raised toward the ceiling, announcing a toast in Italian which nobody could understand. Yet no matter. *There proves no significance to the language of such toasts, for they all mean the same. All words chosen for the expression easily translated as: I'm glad that we are here, I'm glad that we are together. Here, together.*

Cole

He followed her with his eyes until she disappeared into the café. He shivered as the wind came down off the mountain, watching the breeze ripple the sea as if a whisper had passed upon the water. Then across the field of stone and sage, approaching the garden where Mr. and Mrs. Kappatos sat watching evening's farewell.

"How was the nap?" Cole asked.

"Fine," Mr. Kappatos said, a tumbler of wine hanging loosely in his hand.

"Wine in kitchen," Mrs. Kappatos said. Cole nodded and hurried into the house, poured himself a glass of the white homemade wine, then returned to the garden. He sat in the grass. The wind fell a moment, and the island became silent, the mild summer air rich with salt and scents of wildflowers. The wine possessed a clean twang, flushing Cole's face, making him want to talk.

"Your goddaughter, Maria," he said. The Kappatoses looked at each other. Cole pointed toward the beach. "I saw her, met her. At the beach. I talk to Maria at beach," he said slowly.

"Good," Mr. Kappatos said, "She knows English."

"Yes," Cole said. "She speaks English well."

"Tomorrow," Cole said, scratching his head, "Tomorrow we go riding in jeep." He pointed at the jeep. "Maria show me places." The Kappatoses looked to each other again. They nodded.

"Good, nice," Mrs. Kappatos said. "You hungry?"

"No ma'am. That lunch filled me full as a tick." Mrs. Kappatos squinted her eyes in confusion. "No thanks," he said, rubbing his stomach, "Full."

Later, after the Kappatoses had gone to play cards with friends, Cole lay on his bed with the lights on, a closed novel resting on his chest. He stared at the ceiling. A single fly flew from one corner of the room to the other. *I know what you're going through there buddy. Don't have a clue of your destination, don't even know which road to take. Just floating through your days, allowing life to happen to you. No plans, no real motives. Just wishing this life could be as easy as it was during school, when everything seemed to matter, time constantly filled with friends and laughter. And Lily. But it looks like it's going to be all right without Lily, if these pretty girls keep crossing your path. Just admit it old boy, Maria's as pretty as they come. Plus you're on an island in the midst of a sea bluer than the Mississippi autumn sky.*

Don't lie and believe that circumstances don't matter. They do. The night you met Lily had its circumstances, although most of that night revolved around whisky. And courage. Whisky and courage, thick as thieves. So this encounter didn't have any whisky, but it had the sea. You don't know it very well, that old endless expanse of water, but you can already tell that it's going to affect you. Gonna have its way with you. Just like Moon Lake. Just like Lily. Just like a group

*of twenty mallard greenheads cupping down through the flooded
timber on a striking December day in the Nixon Creek bottom. Some
sights you just don't stand a chance against. And the sea's not going to
be an exception. Throw Maria into the painting and well, nobody ever
said you were strong in that way. Did they old boy?*

*I'll give it beautiful. No doubt this land pleases the eye. Yet life
itself doesn't feel that different. You are still Cole Morgan, you're only
in Kefalonia now. Funny how the short layover in Athens meant
nothing. You grow up hearing of foreign cities like Athens, Rome,
Johannesburg. From Mississippi the sounds of their names seem magical,
as if traveling there would automatically cause some sort of significant
revelation or enlightenment, when actually their mystery only comes
from being across the sea, and because the countries in which they
reside are sometimes mentioned by the anchormen on the evening news.*

*Yet your own life still haunts you, even in Athens. Yes it's lovely
with its white stone buildings and red roofs, sitting there between the
mountains and sea, and the women possess a strange beauty, and the
stray dogs wander the buildings like ghosts the people cannot see. But
you still have your life, even on a half-hour layover in Athens, Greece.
You still think about Lily and the smell she left every morning on the
right side of your bed. You still think about Will, how he himself had
seemed to fall in love on the very day he left you, swimming with Mimi
all day out by the sandbar, not even paying attention to anyone else.
Sure Mimi was caught up with him being older and all, but I swear*

something was there. Something more, something possible. Potential rode on every word they exchanged. Hope maybe. For all the bullshit lines I heard from that boy's mouth, when he told Mimi on the dock before we left that he'd come see her in Clarksdale, I knew he was telling the truth. When Will spoke sincerely he couldn't hide it. Damn I should have driven. Smitty was right, he never could hold his liquor. But good God he was fun with a tight buzz on. He could make them laugh, every last one of them. Swear he could. Give him a glass of Maker's and water and he'd make life go away for a little while for anyone who wanted to listen.

I didn't cry right there on the road like Smitty did. Smitty lay down on top of him and cried his eyes out. I remember the dirty gravel in the cuts on his arm and how the pavement tore his ear up pretty good. I left Smitty there with Will, walking the half-mile back to Fletcher's cabin where I found everybody inside making sandwiches and laughing about the day. They looked at me, all dusty from the field and blood on my face, and Mary Martha went to her knees. I'll never forget that. You wouldn't think someone would really do that. Only in a movie would someone go to their knees. But I swear it was like Mary Martha lost the power to stand, and I hadn't even said anything yet. Mimi just stood there with a sandwich in her hand, waiting. That's when I lost it. It took ten minutes before my body would allow a word to escape. A few of the girls led me to the couch and just sat there, holding me. They were speaking but I can't remember anything they said, their voices just mumbled tones in a forgotten dream.

Fletcher and the others ran out of the cabin when I lost it, knowing that whatever happened was close if I had walked back that quickly. When I did speak I sounded just like Smitty the other night in Tupelo, "I knew we shouldn't have let him drive, I knew it." But we didn't know it. That's just the power of hindsight. You inject some inhuman quality to yourself after the fact, as if you had some power to overcome the tragedies of this life. You don't, and neither does anyone else. Tragedy is around the corner. Nobody's immune. You thought you were, didn't you old boy? Thought life would always run as smooth as Moon Lake at sunset.

His first night of rest in Kefalonia passed quickly and true, waking to the new shine as if he'd only been asleep a few minutes. There had been no dreams, and Cole felt thankful. Thankful for the absence of thought. He crawled out of the small single bed, opening the drapes and staring at the sea all blue and calm.

He dressed and fetched his shaving kit out of his bag, walked up to the house. In the kitchen he found Mrs. Kappatos slicing tomatoes.

"Good morning, Cole," she said in surprisingly crisp English.

"Morning to you," Cole said.

He pulled his toothbrush and shampoo from his kit, held them aloft.

"Come," she said, "I show." She led him to the bathroom, ushered him in and shut the door behind. The shower was only a bathtub with a long stretch cord attached to a nozzle. There was no curtain. Cole undressed and climbed in, trying to clean his body without spraying water all over the bathroom floor. He got on his knees to shampoo his hair, laughing at himself. He thought about asking Mrs. Kappatos if he was going about this right, but then again thought it would be difficult if not impossible for her to explain hygiene matters in English. He wiped the bathroom floor with a towel and brushed his teeth, then redressed. In the kitchen Mrs. Kappatos had a plate of tomatoes and bread and a saucer of olive oil spread out on the table.

"Breakfast," she said. "I hope you like."

"I'll like," Cole said. He ate, running the bread through the olive oil. Mrs. Kappatos messed around in the kitchen, preparing all sorts of food.

"We eat at three next," she said. "Bring Maria if like. Come at three. I cook food much."

"Where's Mr. Kappatos?" Cole asked.

"Mavrata," she said, thinking how to go on, "We have garden there. Big garden. You go some morning. You help him. He like that."

"Sounds good," Cole said.

He thanked her for the breakfast and went out into the morning. The Katelios valley basked in the new sun. Cole cranked the jeep and headed out the gravel drive to the main road. The air swirled in the truck, and, for a moment, a longing for home descended.

He drove down to the shops at Katelios, parking at the edge of the beach, buying an International Herald from the newsstand. Cole read the headlines while sitting on the front of the jeep, the sea stretching forever before him.

Maria walked down from the café. Cole noticed her hair, black and straight and tucked behind her ears.

"How was your first night of sleep in Kefalonia?"

"Glorious," Cole said, "And free from dreams."

"I've always thought that dreams are more appropriate for the waking hours," Maria said. "Then we can turn them on and off as we please. The night dreams have too much control."

"I'll agree to that."

"I thought we'd just drive all morning and eat lunch on the northern shore. At Fiskardo. You'll love it there, all these cafés against a dock of sailboats and Ithaki just across the water."

"Sounds good. But Mrs. Kappatos said something about lunch at three. And, to invite you."

"Then we'll just drink a glass of wine at Fiskardo and drive back through the interior. Past the church of the patron saint."

"What about your café?" Cole said, "No hostess at lunch?"

"I have my little cousin Thalia to fill in. She's helped me before."

"Why?"

"Why what?"

"Why take a day off for a strange boy you've talked to for ten minutes?"

"Pity."

"I accept pity."

"Good," she said.

They passed few cars on the road to Argostoli, the villages of Platiae and Simotata and Vlachata seemingly barren save a few old men upon benches, conversing, watching the jeep pass without a wave as if nothing more than a bird, the wind. Maria spoke of the villages, cousins who lived in each, slices of the past that she attributed to different stretches of road. Cole listened and watched the sea as if it might disappear if he looked away.

"Is that blue?" he asked.

"Yes, that's blue," Maria answered.

"How often would y'all go to Argostoli when you were growing up?"

"Hardly ever," Maria said. "The fruit and bread trucks delivered to Father's café every day. Plus, we didn't have a car until I was twelve."

"Lie?"

"I'm serious," Maria said, "My uncle Spiro had a car that Father could use if necessary, but we didn't have one of our own. Why would we need one?"

"Trips."

"Trips? Did you see what Katelios looks like? Why would you want to go somewhere else?"

"You did," Cole said.

"That was different. That was about education."

"You needed an English professor to say you were smart?"

Maria looked down at her lap. "No, stranger, but I did need surroundings where people wanted to learn. Sometimes there's not much desire to know about the world here in Kefalonia."

Cole offered his hand, palm up. Maria slapped it.

"Don't ever let me tease you," Cole said.

"Why not?"

"Because I didn't have the courage to go anywhere else."

"Is this going to be one of those conversations that people who've only known each other for one day are not supposed to have?" Maria asked.

"Yes."

"Good. Just so I know. I'm not trying to act like going to England was brave. I just went. And besides, you're here, right? Now you've gone somewhere else."

"Forced."

"By whom?"

"My folks."

"Why?"

Cole looked back at the sea. It was still there and it provided no comfort or answer or clue. It even clouded the question: how a boy from Mississippi finds himself in a jeep with a Greek girl all lovely and dark and making him feel similar to how Lily made him feel on those drives to Sardis Lake. *Scary, isn't it old boy? To know that someone might make you feel as Lily did. You knew it was possible, you just didn't want to admit it. Thought it would somehow disgrace Lily in your own mind. You wanted to protect her immortality, protect the sincerity of your sadness in regards to losing her. Finding someone else would take away your excuse to be sad, your reason to* long for her. At least you can still be sad about Will, bud. A girl can't take that away. You've got a right to that despair.

"They wanted me to get away."

"From what?" Maria said.

"A lot of things, stranger."

"Is that how you feel? That I'm a stranger?"

"No."

"How does that happen? How do you know one person all your life and still not want to tell them anything and then you know another for one day and want to tell them everything?"

"I try to stay away from those questions without answers."

"But they're the most fun," Maria said.

"And most despairing."

"Do you discuss emotion this casually with all people you meet?" Maria said.

"Only lovely Greek girls."

Maria laughed and touched Cole's forearm where it lay on the console. She left her hand there a moment, then squeezed his skin softly as she looked out over the Kefalonian morning. *It can happen this fast, so don't act so damn surprised at your heart. Remember the other night with the Kara girl, the entire experience a few hours. So you're in another country and the sea is all blue and endless and there's a mountain out your guest house window that sits mythically above the water, that's nothing but drama. The sea doesn't have anything to do with how her fingers felt on your arm. It would have felt the same out at Billy's camp house in Yazoo City, or the sand bar at Moon Lake, or sitting on a stool up at the Grocery. They've touched your arm at those places, and it felt just as good. Don't try and use unique to justify the old muscle in your chest. It doesn't need justification. It does as it wishes. She touched your arm and you liked it, old bud, Greece or no Greece.*

You're just starting to forget now, so Lily doesn't have as much hold on you. You're getting yourself freed up, old boy, loosening the ropes from the dock. Someone else will move into that slot and that's the way it is for you and everyone else, so don't get noble and think every girl gets her own damn storage room. You can't preserve them like that, bud, and it wouldn't do anybody any good if you could. Think about the fishing trips with your grandfather. He does get his own storage room. Hell, the image of the old man's scarred hands trying to tie a fly on a trout leader gets its own damn room by itself. You've got to write about him more, Cole, you owe him that much. You ought to write about that afternoon at Cypress Hole when the bottom fell out of the sky.

He looked up at the interior mountain Ainos, the dry rocky terrain along the roadside. It's just another place. Foreign means nothing now. I always thought life would appear different in another country, that some sort of extraordinary objectivity could be attained. Books have made you silly, old bud. Sure this place has the sea and good bread delivered every morning and tomatoes dipped in olive oil, and sure it has a pretty dark haired girl named Maria that touches your arm at exactly the right time and makes you feel wanted, special, but this place doesn't have any answers, nor, I bet, does any other. If a place possessed the answers then we could all live there, and everyone would have it all figured out, and nobody would have to converse except deciding on what to eat for supper or what to do in the afternoons, and there wouldn't be any need for books or writing because there's no need to ask the questions if the answers are at your fingertips. See, bud, you're going about this all wrong. The answers are on the other side of the river, and for now, you've got to take care of your days on this side. So just live on this side right now, and quit asking the questions that can only be answered on the other.

You don't have to explain everything to yourself either. You can simply be happy that Maria touched your arm and sad that Lily's in Boston living out her dream and probably curled up with some thespian in the sack. You can feel these emotions without discussing them within. Remember: I hurt, I love, I long.

"Can I ask you a broad, silly, unanswerable question?" Maria said.

"Absolutely."

"What's home like?"

"America or Mississippi?" Cole said.

"They're the same, aren't they?"

"Not at all. In fact, sometimes America doesn't even claim us."

"Don't be silly."

"I'm serious."

"Why would you say that?" Maria said.

"Folks up east that hadn't ever been bitten by a Delta mosquito think they understand the south."

"You're confusing me," Maria said.

"Okay. Did folks in England know what life was like in Kefalonia?"

"No."

"Did they act like they knew?"

"No."

"Well, everybody thinks they know what Mississippi is all about."

"Yeah," Maria said, "But England's another country. It's different."

"It's not different. It's the same principle. Folks acting like they understand a place they've never lived in. I hate it when people act like they understand Mississippi when they've never seen an October cotton field in Holly Ridge or the sun go down over the river levee at Moon Lake."

They descended the last stretch of hills into Argostoli, the capital city. Overlooking the bay of Argostoliou, a thumbnail of sea that stretches around the point of Lassi, forming an inland lake, protected from the winds by the hills above the beaches of Makrys Gialos and Platys Gialos. Sailboats and cargo ships rested along the docks where people milled about fruit stands and gift shops and fish markets. Cole eased through the streets, watching folks go about their day.

"Neat town," he said.

"Yeah, it's nice. Turn up here," Maria said, "We'll cross the
bridge and get on the road to Fiskardo. It'll carry us up on the
mountain and you'll be able to look back across the bay and see
Argostoli from above."

Cole turned upon the narrow bridge that lay level with the
water as if the stone floated upon the sea. Fishermen sat on the
stone ramparts, bait fishing the shallows. All had black hair and
olive skin and eyes that Cole believed held stories he'd like to hear.
He always made time for others who fished. Something about a
fisherman's words possessed a deeper meaning to him, a disguised
offer of friendship, even if the conversation only contained advice
about what color jig to use for crappie at North Lake or what size
sowbug to use below the dam on the Little Red. Sometimes the
simplest exchanges meant most to the boy, little secrets of a trade
that he'd known since birth.

He would always remember the joy he felt one Sunday morning
at church, in his early youth, when the minister's sermon constantly
referred to the disciples as fishermen, how excited he was that the
first believers of his faith made their living upon the water. Never
had he known peace as when fishing a farm lake with his grandfather in a fourteen foot johnboat that leaked a tad in the rear, a
red Folger's can there for the occasional bail. Often times when

the fish were slow Cole would set his rod down and watch the old man, the rhythm of his casts, how he would never hurry his retrieve, considering his placement a moment before throwing the lure. The old man possessed a natural method to his fishing, and the stories he told while on the lake seemed to mesh with the actual movements of rod and wrist and line and lure to create a dramatic performance of sorts. As if the old man had choreographed the entire scene. Actually, he'd just been doing it for a good long while, over sixty years, and holding a rod had become as natural and familiar as holding his wife, who had gone on to her reward before Cole was born, and in her loss the sincerity and grace of their relationship transferred to what the old man had left, a grandson who loved to fish as much as he.

"What are you thinking about so hard?" Maria said.

"Too much to say. Or maybe nothing."

"That's helpful." Maria gave him a playful nudge on the arm then turned her sights back across the bay where you could see Argostoli and the villages of Lixouri and Agios Dimitrios.

"Is it beautiful?" Maria said.

"It's beautiful," he said. Cole looked at her face as she stared out over the bay. For the first time he sincerely noticed her features: the stone-colored skin, the straight black hair blowing across her face, three freckles that dotted her left cheek in a crescent moon of sorts. Her lips were thin, only a tint darker than her skin. She wore a white blouse unbuttoned at the top, sleeves rolled up, silver spec sunglasses that hid the intent of her eyes. She was quite striking to Cole, although this realization didn't happen at first. Her beauty wasn't the sort you recognized on the street. It had to be coupled with the relevance of her words and the soft, mild pitch of her voice. And, of course, the way she touched you on the arm when you said something witty. *There's no reason to be surprised, the times you have fallen you fell this quickly. Look at the night you met Lily. You just can't get over the circumstances of this one, can you old boy? The champions of fate would be cheering this one, but you really don't buy that, do you? This life is simply a series of days, and if you live enough of them you're going to cross paths with people that you find attractive, that you enjoy listening to, that you want to touch in the evenings. There's nothing special about finding someone. Only the keeping.*

You ought to write all this down. A fine essay it would make. You always thought you didn't have anything to write about but you always did, just didn't recognize the value of it all. Well, if you don't recognize Will and Maria as worth writing about, then you really don't have a prayer, do you? You might as well only read. Everyone's not supposed to write, this life couldn't handle such. But you are and you know it. If it wasn't right then it wouldn't hurt you so damn much. Quit denying the pen and realize that Will won't be there when you get back and damn it, care for this Maria girl if you want to. Lily doesn't need your protection anymore.

And don't give in to any drama. Folks back home would call it dramatic because you're in Kefalonia and there's a sea that defines blue. But this isn't drama. It's unique because Mississippi boys don't usually travel to islands in the Ionian Sea. But if they did, they'd surely meet the girls and the girls would love their strangeness. So just because your old man has the money to get you here, don't think you have a right to any drama. Drama is the last words of a dying man or a boat caught in a thunderstorm or a fifteen foot putt to win the Open championship. Meeting a girl doesn't have anything to do with drama. You're supposed to meet girls. In Kefalonia or Tupelo, no matter. Leave the drama to Gibson and the Dodgers. They're better at it than you are.

"Silence won't do us any good," Maria said, interrupting Cole from his thoughts.

"Translate, please."

"Well, how long are you staying?"

"Two weeks," Cole said.

"Two weeks for a lifetime," she said. "See, every minute you sit over there grinding thoughts you miss getting to know me that much better."

"You're arguing against yourself," he said.

"How so?"

"Well if it's two weeks for a lifetime, then what's the point?"

"I didn't know we were going to be hurtful," she responded.

"You're the one who said two weeks for a lifetime. I've never heard a more despairing sentence."

"Well, okay then. How about, you never know."

"I've never had much luck with, you never know," Cole said.

"So you've used it before."

"Yes."

"It's just a way out, isn't it?" she said.

"Yes."

"Then to hell with it."

"Hello," Cole said.

"I cuss when I get frustrated," Maria said.

"You cuss beautifully and surprisingly."

"What a noble talent to have," she said.

"Okay," he said, "Let's get to know you. Tell me about England."

"England is green and civilized and the clouds continue as if they have no other choice."

"Was there a boy?"

"There were many boys," she said, "The English reproduce with the same outcome as Greeks and Americans."

"Again I ask, was there a boy?"

"Yes. A boy there was."

"Good. Now, a name, please."

"Why?" Maria said.

"Without a name I can't formulate stereotypes or generalizations."

"Oh, well then, his name was Keane."

"Did you think he hung the moon?"

"At one time."

"Someone must always hang the moon," Cole said.

"Not in England," she said, "The clouds render the moon useless."

"She's a poet," he said.

They turned on a stretch of road along the steep cliffs of the western coast of the island. The sea lay several hundred feet below, calm and green-blue in the mid-morning sun. The distant sky met the water, as if it was all enclosed. This world, this life. The mild wind blew against Cole's face, and he drove slowly without any intent of ever arriving at a destination.

"There was no real end to it," Maria said after a few minutes of silence.

"To what?"

"Oh, you're real interested."

"I'm sorry," he said, "Keane, there was no real end to Keane."

"We simply left," Maria said. "We never talked about anything. We just lived up until graduation and then we said goodbye. As if we both knew we weren't ready to make decisions."

"What decisions?"

"I don't know. Whether to live in the same place, for example. Someone must always change their plans, you know."

"Exactly. That's why any decision that constitutes complete sacrifice between young people is impossible. Nobody wants to give in because they fear regret. Older folks don't worry about regret like the young do, because they've already experienced enough of it."

"Tell me how you feel," Maria said.

"I'm serious."

"I agree with what you said but it has to be worded differently. You can't use the word impossible, difficult is more appropriate. Dealing with decisions requiring complete sacrifice is not impossible, it's difficult. That's the problem with English-speaking boys. They butcher the moments that require the most eloquence."

"And the Greeks handle it like poets."

"No," Maria said, "They simply say nothing. Complete silence. As if ignored, the sun would go away. But most often silence is less frustrating. Silence hurts but incompetent words hurt and make you angry. Pain and anger tend not to be promising for the boy."

"Affirmed."

"Experience?"

"Yes," Cole said, "I've created my fair share of pain and anger. But usually only in the end. I always flourish in the beginning. Of course Will had to get me in the door a few times."

"Who is Will?"

"A friend, a best friend."

"In the door?" Maria said.

"You know, over to our table at a bar, anything like that. I need a wingman at first, but then I'm good to go."

"This is getting a bit procedural."

"I'm amazed at your English," Cole said, "You'd do fine in Mississippi. Might need a little help with the sayings, but you'd do fine."

"The sayings?"

"The slang," he said, "Like, 'This hamburger's good as a government check.'"

"What does that mean?"

"See, you'd need some help with the sayings. Folks in the south like to use sayings every other sentence. If you're not from there you can get lost quickly."

"Tell me another."

"Fine as frog hair split three ways."

"Again."

"Three sheets to the wind."

"I give up."

"Don't worry, I'd translate for you."

"Is that an invitation?" Maria said.

"You don't need one. Mississippi allows Greeks."

"You avoided that one rather quickly."

"I'm only playing," he said.

She would look lovely on the sand bar at Moon Lake. I wonder what she'd think of it all. It's not Kefalonia, but something tells me she'd appreciate it. Fletcher and Smitty sure would get a kick out of it. Of course this is all assuming that Moon Lake is even the same, now that it represents the day of Will's death. You haven't been back since that day and you're a bit scared, aren't you, old boy? Scared that it's changed, that no longer will it represent the utter freedom of your youth, that the sunsets will now bring you despair and longing for Will when before it brought you such peace. To watch that southern sun drop down all blood red behind the levee, leaving faint streaks of pink across the Delta sky. Maybe it will become your pilgrimage, the high-ways and back roads between Oxford and Moon Lake, and you'll feel a constant desire to return, for Will's sake, because you know that's what he would want.

Aw, listen to you getting all noble and dramatic. Nothing's going to change. You'll go to Moon Lake if you hear the Clarksdale girls are there and you'll go if the crappie are biting around the piers and you'll go if Perry Carter brings his party boat down from Tunica. It won't have anything to do with Will's death. Sure you may think of him and even get one of those tight throats when you drive past the gravel where y'all found him, and when you walk down Fletcher's pier you may see Will kissing Mimi, you may hear him promising her things, but none of it will have anything to do with why you came. The memory of him

will simply be with you, just as he was with you before. Will's not going
anywhere, you just can't slap his palm anymore.

"Returning to the point," Maria said, "You're saying that once
the time comes where a decision must be made, then it's much
easier to simply leave."

"Yes."

"Take me back to the café please."

"Maria," Cole said, smiling, reaching out and taking hold of
her wrist, "I didn't say it was the right thing to do. I said it was
the easiest."

"It sounds like it's what you'd do."

"Actually, in furtherance of our free emotional setting, it was
done to me."

"I don't believe it," Maria said.

"There, you see, you're taking my feelings for granted because
I'm a boy from the American south. In the entire world we're the
only people not allowed to possess feelings." Maria laughed.

"Okay then, who was the girl?"

The girl, she asks. I don't really know anymore. Like some dream
I had several nights ago, still familiar yet lacking true reality, as if
unsure that our year together even happened. There was a point
where I thought I'd found the girl everyone had talked about all my life,
"The right one for me." If this life has ever known a lie, it's when someone
says to you, "Someday you'll find that one person right for you." I've

already found two and I'm not even looking. And then when you do decide, people say, "I'm so happy that you found the right person for you." I hope I've been drinking whisky when some old blue blood friend of Mama says that to me, because I'm going to sip from my Maker's and water and return with, "No ma'am, there were plenty right for me, I just picked the one that would make love to me in the morning."

Listen to you old bud, you're just bitter because Lily did the leaving. And don't think you're keeping your pain hid very well. Folks know. And they know it's not all about Will. You heard Smitty, asking if you thought about Lily. You don't think Smitty Cook can read your mind. Your fishing partners read you like an open book. Must be something in the way you cast.

"Lily, her name was Lily."

"You don't have to go on," Maria said, "Just because we're not acting like strangers doesn't mean you have to tell all."

"I know," Cole said. "It's fine."

They both looked out over the sea. The road ahead hung on the side of the mountain and in the distance a string of grey clouds moved across the sky, creating shadows on the water. It was nearing noontime and Cole felt his back sweating against the seat. The wind warm on his face. *A fine highway, a fine girl. What's so strange about that? Because we're in Kefalonia? Anything dramatic or special about this is just the sea's fault, because it's so damn blue. Just imagine that you're riding out Old Taylor Road on the way*

to eat catfish and you'll do just fine. Don't do Lily any favors because
you're in Kefalonia. Tell it like it happened, in Mississippi.

"She wanted to be an actress," Cole said, "Sounds silly, doesn't
it. Kind of like I wanted to play shortstop for the Braves."

"The Braves?"

"You know, the Atlanta Braves. A pro-baseball team."

"Yes, you playing baseball is silly but her wanting to be an
actress is not."

"Appreciate that."

"You're welcome. Where did she go?"

"Boston," Cole said, "To theatre school."

"Maybe she'll become famous."

"Whose side are you on?" Cole said.

"I wasn't aware that I had to choose."

"No, you're not supposed to choose. You're simply supposed
to be on my side even if I'm wrong because you're riding shotgun
in my jeep. State law in Mississippi requires a girl riding shotgun
on a country road to be on the boy's side."

"I don't think they apply Mississippi law in Kefalonian
courts."

Cole grinned. "Anyway, it was different than you and Keane.
Sounds like, anyway. We talked too much. Talked the whole
thing right into the ground."

"Let me ask you something," Maria said. "At the end, did she always look like she was waiting on you to say something else, no matter how much you said?"

"What are you trying to ask me?" Cole said.

"If you would have asked her to stay..."

"No, it wouldn't have mattered. She was going anyway."

"Then it doesn't matter," Maria said.

"Yeah, well, it doesn't make it any easier. Whisky's the only thing that makes it easier. The good ole Maker's bite. Make you slap your mama."

"You know, you could have asked her anyway, just to make her happy. Just to let her know that's what you were thinking."

"You're no different," Cole said, "You know that."

"What do you mean?"

"I swear, nothing surprises me anymore. You could have fooled me. I would have thought two girls from different corners of the map might differ."

"What are you talking about?" Maria said.

"I'm talking about what you just said, about telling her that I wanted her to stay just for her own sake. Sounds like something straight from Lily's mouth."

"You were in love with this girl, weren't you?"

"Don't do that."

"Do what?" Maria said.

"Ask questions like that after I lose it. Makes me feel like I'm wearing my heart on my sleeve."

"Well you are."

"Yeah, well, you don't have to remind me. It's charming to wear your heart on your sleeve if you don't know you're doing it, but if you know then it's just pitiful."

"Sometimes girls like pitiful better than charming," Maria said.

"Yeah," Cole said, "Well here I am."

They walked along the docks at Fiskardo — moored sailboats bearing flags from other countries, cafés where tourists ate lunch and drank wine in the mild sun. Across the straight of Daskalio the mountain island of Ithaki rose into the afternoon sky.

Maria walked just ahead of him, pointing out the shops, voicing tidbits of the village's history. Only the shopkeepers were Greek, the rest a collage of tourists. Cole heard several languages as they strolled past the outside tables of the cafés. At the end of the dock Maria chose a table next to the water's edge and ordered a carafe of wine in Greek.

They remained silent several minutes, sipping their wine, smiling at each other, feeling the breeze coming off the straight. *It's a very pleasant and okay time to be quiet, now, with that island rising into the sky like that. It would be irreverent to discuss reality in the presence of that sight. But wine and silence do it justice. It would be a fine place to tell a girl that you loved her, but only for the first time. Once you've spoken those words then it matters not where you are when you tell her again. For life allows a bit of drama on that first time, and if you're a wise enough cat to combine that drama with a special place, well then, you've secured a memory, at least for the girl. It's only a memory for you if the words are true. Hopefully you'd keep them to yourself if they aren't, but we all surprise ourselves once in awhile.*

Often times the whisky helps with those lies, both with their creation and justification.

You can think of a few other places, too, can't you old bud, where you'd like to surprise a girl with the words everyone wants to hear. Of course out at the sandbar at Moon Lake, mid-September maybe, evening, a sunset involved. The cotton fields south of Greenville in late fall, before they start to picking, rows of white fluff running towards timberlines painted in crimson oaks. Even Memphis, down by the river, when they bring the city orchestra to the banks to welcome summer home.

Lily stole that moment from you, and in a way, you've always held it against her. Granted you've never been in a hurry with your emotions, but you still felt betrayed when she said it first. Should have known an actress would beat you to the punch. December, wasn't it old boy, and y'all had both finished your exams. Drove out to Sardis with a bottle of red wine, late afternoon, the woods bare and grey. Pulled up to the beach as a north wind sent white caps against the shore, the first bitter cold of the southern winter. You left the heat running and Lily crawled over into your lap and y'all kissed between sips of the chalky wine. You remember how her mouth tasted clean and nice from the wine. And you thought about telling her right then, in fact you'd thought about it several times before, even as far back as the last football games. But you had decided to wait until the warmth came again, some afternoon in early spring. You thought the anticipation of it would make it better, memorable.

And then she just came on with it right there in the truck. Said that she wanted you to know exactly how she felt. Said that you possessed her now in the best and worst possible way. In that way that leaves only two outs: a broken heart or a full one. But that she thought the risk of a broken heart far more honorable than the careful prevention of one. Said she believed love the appropriate word now, took a deep breath, waited a moment for your response, then stated she needed another drink if you weren't going to say anything. "I love you, too," you had said, and felt the failure in your chest.

"Where do you go?" Maria said.

"What?"

"Where do you go?"

"I'm not sure I understand," Cole said.

"A moment ago," Maria said, "You weren't in Kefalonia. You were somewhere else."

"Nonsense."

"No reason to hide it. I do it too, just not usually in the company of other people."

"It's my only flaw," Cole said.

"I imagine I could spot a few more, that is, if we continue our friendship."

"I'm sure you could, and, was that a confirmation?"

"A confirmation?" she said.

"Of our friendship?"

"I didn't know such was necessary."

"Me neither. But you said it, I don't know, with purpose."

"Don't worry, southern boy. I'm not going to make you sign anything. I don't carry obligations with my friendship."

"No obligation for honesty?" Cole said, "Or loyalty? How about sympathy?"

"Those qualities are inherent in Greeks, my friend. Only Americans have to acquire such traits."

"I set you up for that one."

"And I converted."

"Your English amazes me," he said.

"Don't be cute," Maria said, "It affects my sarcasm when I find a boy cute."

She is lovely, sitting there with the water so blue behind her and the tourist families strolling by and the table umbrellas rattling in the slight breeze coming across the straight from Ithaki. But every time you find a girl lovely it tends to end poorly, usually of your own accord. It would be nice to find a girl lovely for a good long while and every-thing be all potential and hope. You hope for a very long time and then, when you get what you've been hoping for, you realize how much more beautiful it was when it was only hope. Words and actions end our lit-tle paintings of how this life is supposed to unfold.

"I'm surprised my godparents didn't say something to you

about our trip to Fiskardo," Maria said.

"Come again?"

"I guess you would call it 'old fashioned' back in the States. Girls aren't supposed to make a habit of riding around the island with strange boys."

"Seriously?"

"Seriously. In fact, boys usually only court girls at their homes if they are engaged. But my godparents have always been easy-going."

"What about your folks?" Cole said.

"They won't have much to say."

"Why?"

"They're gone."

"Gone?"

"The permanent kind, Cole. Gone."

"What do I say?" Cole said.

"You say nothing, my friend. I can see in your face that you're sorry for me and I appreciate it and that's the end of it. Now let's get some more wine."

Maria motioned the waiter toward the empty carafe. He returned with a new one. Maria poured Cole another glass and they sat in silence, the appropriate kind of silence after something intimate has been said and the faculties need a moment to cool down. *The cooling down always helps with the bitter taste of wine or the bite of Maker's. Now and always. The best whisky you ever had,* old bud, was after Mama called to say that your grandfather had gone on to his reward. Quickly, she said, a stroke. You'd been fishing with him up on the Little Red just two weeks before and then he was gone. You walked into the den and told Smitty. "Let's go get a drink," Smitty said. It was late afternoon at the Grocery, and y'all went out on the porch and watched the people walk by on the Square. Smitty sat and listened as you told all the fishing stories about your grandfather, and the Maker's was curling your lip and flushing your face and you got it all out. Realize how much you owe friends when you look back on it all, don't you bud. Death isn't so bad when you have a tumbler of Maker's, a friend, and fishing stories to tell.

Don't ask Maria about her folks. She'll tell you when she's good and ready. Surprised she even mentioned it. She must like you. But don't push it. Girls don't like to talk of the biggies until they've touched you. And sometimes not until they've touched you a while. You may not deserve to know on this trip. But you let her decide that. It's her right.

They drove back to Katelios through the central part of the
island, climbing the interior mountains, the road painting the
edges of outcroppings where you could peer out over the noon sea.
They dropped into valleys of grape fields and olive trees, passing
through tiny villages where Cole thought, *these folks are unaware
that a world is going on out there. Unencumbered, content. Will I ever
feel that way again?*

Wildflowers bloomed in the valley of the patron saint
Gerasimos. They parked along the roadside and walked up
through the courtyard between the church and convent. Liturgy
could be heard through the open doors of the convent and Cole
wandered into a small sanctuary where nuns sat in cubicles reading.
Visitors blessed the several shrines. In the corner lay the tomb of
the patron saint. Cole stood before it, staring. As if something
might occur. He exited to Maria smelling the roses in the gardens
along the brick walkway.

"Well?"

"It's very dark," Cole said.

"You've never been in a convent?"

"Correct. Far from it I'm afraid."

"You've got to smell the roses."

"That's a saying in the States."

"Saying or not, give them a smell," she said.

Walking back to the jeep, Cole stopped and looked at the church. He envisioned the workers who'd created it, brick by brick; men who probably never gave a thought to the unique drama of their work: to build a structure of promise, amidst a valley of grape fields and olive trees, upon an island mountain that rises out of a sea as blue and endless as the sky it mirrors.

"C'mon," Maria said, "We'll be late for Nouna's meal."

"Nouna?"

"Godmother. Your hostess."

"Ahh," Cole said.

On the drive back a comfortable silence descended, one that confirmed the success of the midday trip; a peace between friends where words have been exhausted, no conclusions necessary, the passing terrain and the shine of the sea a suitable end. *Our notions are comical, especially those of a southern boy who has never left the south. These places my parents traveled didn't seem real to me, as if my life could only unfold along the highways of Mississippi and Tennessee.*

Greece.

Nothing more than a figment of my imagination a week ago. A land on a map. Spoken about on the news sometimes, yet having no effect on the muscle in my chest. Then you throw a girl into the scene, one with black hair tucked behind her ears and the temperament of a saint, and you mix it with this golden, rocky terrain, and you realize that life exists on Kefalonia. And probably elsewhere. That if you traveled to these places and took your meals in the cafés and stayed in the inns that you would meet new people, that you would find things to write about, that experience would transpire that brought tears and laughter, and you'd look up and be living a life. It simply takes this long to realize there's no set itinerary. You don't have to know your destinations, nor the companions you plan to travel with. Such specifics are being handled somewhere else, by someone else. All you can do is wake in the morning and sleep in the night, allowing life to unfold in between. Those who believe they're in control have the least.

Listen to you, old bud, getting a bit high brow. A bit philosophical. Don't start acting like you've got it all figured out simply because life placed a lovely Greek girl upon your path. It's easy to believe in fate when she touches your arm like that and smiles when you attempt to be charming. How difficult fate seemed when Will lay there on the side of the road, the gravel dirtying the cuts upon his back with Smitty lying on top of him, whimpering. Did you appreciate life happening to you that day? Were you a follower of fate at the funeral, when Will's mama tried to get up before the crowd and eulogize her son but couldn't because the pain brought tears so intense that words weren't possible? She had to walk down from the podium without ever getting a sound out, shaking her head, having lost her son and the ability to relate how much she had loved him to the only ones in this world who cared.

You're such a fair weather fan, aren't ya' old bud? Believe in girls when it's easy, believe in fishing when the crappie are biting the jigs inside the levee, believe in fate as long as it doesn't snatch any more buddies. You've got one thing right, the part about living the day. That's all you can do. But as far as knowing why, you've got some years to go and don't think there'll ever be a complete answer. Don't act like you never saw any despair and frustration in the mug of your grandfather. You did, regardless of how beautifully he fished. And that old cat had seventy-five years behind him. If there's doubt at seventy-five then don't be claiming any knowledge at twenty-two, hear? You've read a few books and lost a best friend and now you've been to Greece, so you're getting a little confident about experience. Losing Will didn't make you wise, it made you sad, less whole. Don't confuse emotion with traits they place on war heroes. Courage and wisdom are reserved for those who've been gone at least a decade. They don't have any place on your mantel. That's only life. It's expected of you. If you live with chin held high then you're worthy of competency at most. And you haven't always achieved that, have you Cole boy?

Don't be too rough on yourself. Just come back from being all noble and just be a southern boy again who believes this Greek girl easy on the eyes. You know you could probably touch her now. But I'd wait. The touching always got you in the most trouble, and it wasn't always the thing you remembered. You remember the way she looked at you across a table or the way she ate her spaghetti at the Italian place off the Square or the way she performed her monologues in your bedroom,

in the early hours of morning after y'all had been at the bar with
friends. She was always so passionate about acting after she'd been
drinking. You lying on the bed, listening, laughing, knowing that you'd
be in love with this girl for a good long while, or, although it scared you,
permanently. You're not above the touching; you're not saying that. It's
just that the touching occurs in the present, not the past. The touching
makes the young believe that life is simple.

They ate moussaka and greens and bread dipped in tzaziki for the
afternoon meal, Maria translating between Cole and the Kappatoses
for the sake of conversation. Cole told them about his parents, how
they were doing. He didn't know when they'd return to Kefalonia
again, but after seeing it, he imagined very soon. He told about
Mississippi, about Oxford and school, about the terrain this time of
year. How he and his friends did a good bit of fishing in summer. Mr.
Kappatos said that he'd take Cole out on his boat one morning, to go
after some synagrida. Cole nodded and grinned, as he always did upon
an offer to fish. Something about fishing returned him to the mindset
of a small boy, always, even just talk of it, and in those moments he felt
free from all the questions he couldn't answer. He explained freshwater
bass fishing to Mr. Kappatos, and fly-casting for rainbows up on the
Little Red in Arkansas. Maria translated patiently as they went into
specifics about bait and rods and line. Depth. The right kind of
weather. Mrs. Kappatos caught Maria's eye and winked.

"They've forgotten us," she said.

He wrote by lamplight, the wind coming from the open window, the curtains dancing. Only about Will. For his own sake. Writing it down was the only thing that kept him from feeling helpless.

He wrote about the rice field along the Tallahatchie River, the morning he and Will and Smitty knocked down thirty green-heads in the snow, ice hanging from the flanks of Will's yellow retriever Baby. It hadn't snowed in three years, and the boys couldn't imagine a finer place to watch it fall. White powder covered the levees around the field. It melted as it hit the rippling floodwater, a north wind blowing over the top of the pit blind. The mallards came in front-and-center, wings cupped tight, red legs outstretched to light. The boys quit shooting after a while, unloaded their shotguns, poured cups of coffee out of Smitty's thermos. They watched the ducks descend, drove after drove. Baby whimpered as the mallards lit within twenty feet of her, Smitty comforting the retriever, "Stay, old girl. You've had your fun. Just let em' have it."

After a while Smitty let her come in off the dog perch, and she curled up on the floor of the blind, licking her forelegs in front of the charcoal bucket, the ice melting from her coat. The snow fell for hours, the boys staying well past noon talking about girls, about steel versus lead shot, about what they were going to do for the rest of their lives. At one point Will rose and stared out at the white countryside, a flock of specklebelly geese calling their arrival from high above. He spoke without turning to his friends, as if addressing the land, "Possibly the finest morning that I've lived."

He wrote of the bonfire they built out on the beach at Sardis, the last night before everyone went home for the holidays, first semester of their freshman year. How they'd only told a few people about it, the word spreading until several hundred faces stood shivering around the fire, all the boys collecting wood from the forest, building the flame higher and higher until it rose twenty feet into the December night. Embers ascending toward the stars. Pretty girls kneeling with hands outstretched to the warmth, drinking red wine out of water bottles, bumping into friends in the darkness, slapping hands, arms around each other's necks.

Come dawn he and Will and Smitty were still telling stories around the last warmth of the grey dying wood, a few other stragglers holding on with them, fighting sleep, all watching a cold sun rise over the pine hills in the distance. Somebody had gone to town and picked up a mess of ham biscuits, and they all ate furiously as if they'd been stranded for days. One stranger said he'd remember this night always, no matter where the road took him.

He wrote about the girls, the ones who'd fallen for Will. How they'd fallen so quickly, without hesitation. How Will's companionship somehow brought hope, although nobody could ever explain why.

Cole wrote about the year he spent the holidays in the Delta, at Will's family's place a few miles south of Greenville. There hadn't been much rain that year, few fields flooded. Will knew of an old slough inside the levee that held water year around, a slash of buckbrush and cypress that he'd seen mallards pitch in before. The slough stayed hot for two weeks straight, Will and Cole bagging a limit each morning at sunrise, then driving the ten minutes back to Will's place where his mama would have biscuits and sawmill gravy waiting on the table. Then they'd drive the barren cotton fields, talking about the morning hunt, Will pointing out places on the farm where he'd killed a big deer or where they'd planted a sunflower field for doves. Where he'd made love in the back of a pickup in high school. Cole only went home for Christmas day, returning to the Delta right after a family supper at his parents' house. Cole saw the hurt in his mama's eyes that Christmas night. He saw her realize, as she watched his truck back down the driveway, that his heart was somewhere else.

But he wanted to get back. To the mallards and the frosty sunrises along the river. To the smell of bottomland at nightfall. To Will and Smitty, brothers he'd never had. And one, although ignorant of it then, he wouldn't have for long.

He wrote of Elsie, the South African student Will dated during the spring of their sophomore year. She was a visiting political science student studying the similar struggles that Mississippi and South Africa shared in dealing with their troubled history. Their attempts at change; at healing wounds between people. Elsie often said racial hate could be erased like writing on a chalkboard. Smitty would shake his head, suggest that things aren't that easy in Mississippi. Elsie thought such an excuse weaker than silence.

Will had dodged all accusations of commitment from Cole, saying that Elsie's return to South Africa once summer came would be the end, their time together simply remembered for what it was worth. But Cole saw a sincerity in Will's fondness for Elsie that hadn't been present with the other girls, some kind of elevated attention. *I guess you'd call it captivation,* he wrote. And it was far from one-sided. Elsie loved the afternoon fishing trips, the nights camped out on the bluff at Clear Creek. She loved listening to them talk about lures and water temperature and why the crappie would be moving up the creek beds out past Betty Davis country store. And although a bit shy, Elsie, with Smitty begging her over a few cold beers, would tell of South Africa, about the mountains on the sea, about her father taking her to the northern game reserves every year to see the lions. She told of her family, of her father's position in the government, of the expectations placed upon her after her sisters' academic accomplishments in

Europe. She admitted her newfound love of the American south.

"Then why go back?" Smitty said, "Why not stay here?"

"Because it's my home," she explained, "Nothing erases where you're from. Nothing. Besides, I'm eager to see my country change."

One morning that May Will drove Elsie to Memphis to catch her flight home. When he returned to Oxford he found Cole and Smitty sitting in lawn chairs on the front porch, chewing sunflower seeds and watching Baby tear up an old tennis shoe.

"Well, bud," Smitty said, "You look all right. Considerin'."

"I don't feel all right," Will replied.

"You're not supposed to," Cole said, "If you felt all right I'd call you a cold son of a bitch."

"Y'all take me fishing," Will said.

They went to Smitty's farm lake outside Holly Springs, worm fishing the bottom for largemouths. They fished in silence out of some uncomfortable respect for Elsie's departure. Will landed a seven pounder, and without a word removed the hook and released the fish off the back of the boat. Smitty just looked at Cole and shook his head. Come dusk, with the shadows of the shore pines stretched out over the lake, Will spoke: "Can't believe I let her go."

"Yeah," Smitty said, "That's the biggest lunker I've ever seen taken out of this lake."

"He's not talking about the bass, meathead," Cole said.

"If I don't ever find another one," Will said, "If I come to the end of my days a lonely old cat, at least I'll know it was my fault. That I had it and let it go."

Cole stared blankly at the wall. The mild wind rose goose bumps on his arms. Life felt void of time. He put his pen to paper once more: *In the end it's all we have left, little pieces of a life lived hanging around in our memories. I hope the day never comes that I can't recount times shared with Will, but I know, like all things, my remembrances of him will become faded, that I won't recall how many mallards we bagged or crappie caught, or the words said over a campfire on the bluff at Sardis. All I'll remember is the place, and that we were together. In a place, together. Maybe in the end that's all our memories desire.*

He put his journal away, threw on some blue jeans and work boots and walked out into the clear Ionian night. A full moon hung low in the sky, making the world white, the only stars visible those on the dark distant edge of the sea. Cole made his way through the grassy fields to the edge of the village, quiet now, sleeping. He knew where Maria lived. She'd pointed her cottage out when they first left Katelios that morning on the high road to Mavrata. He snuck down the main street past the newspaper stand and the cafés. The sea lapped softly against the stony beach, the lights of Zachynthos twinkling against the black outline of the island.

For a moment Cole felt like a child again, when he and the

neighborhood boys would play hide-and-seek after curfew, sneaking out of their old aristocratic midtown homes and meeting at the lake in Chickasaw Gardens, breaking up into teams, chasing each other through the quiet oak-shaded streets until dawn, the hum of the city somewhere in the distance. *When you're a child, the only time your heart beats with passion is when doing something that can get you into trouble, or something where someone can get hurt. I guess we stay children all our lives.*

The window was open as he'd expected, the moon providing enough light to watch her sleep. She had pushed the covers away, and lay with her hands tucked up under the pillow. Cole stared at her for several minutes before speaking. He whispered her name loudly, then again. She sat up a bit startled, then rubbed her eyes patiently once knowing.

"If they caught you they'd tie a stone to your ankle and drop you in the sea halfway to Zachynthos."

"I'll take my chances," he said. She rose and slipped into her sandals and crawled over the sill.

They sat in the grass, leaning their backs against the stone wall of the cottage. Both stared at the sky. Cole picked a blade and began to chew its end.

"Why'd you come?" Maria said.

"Life's too short to sleep."

"I disagree," she said, "We ought to sleep more. Sometimes

the less we're conscious, the less harm we can do."

"You've never done any harm," Cole said.

"To the contrary, my friend."

"I don't believe it," he said.

"Does it take a very long time to become close to someone?"

"I used to think so," Cole said.

"Is that a no?"

"Maybe," he said, "I'm not sure how to define 'close' anymore."

Maria reached and touched Cole's forearm as she did that morning in the jeep.

"Today was nice," she said.

"It was," he said, looking again to the sky. Maria leaned her cheek against Cole's shoulder. With eyes closed she kissed the sleeve of his shirt.

"We don't need to be having this conversation," she said, "And you need to let me rest. Some of us have to be adults tomorrow." She rose and climbed back in the window. Cole hadn't moved. Maria reached out of the window and tussled his hair.

"Go to sleep, southern boy. Come find me tomorrow after siesta. We can play together awhile."

"Yes ma'am," he said without turning his head. Maria retreated back to her bed.

Cole started back through town, then into the white fields leading to the guest house. A boulder lay along one of the fence lines and Cole sat on it, looking out over the moonlit sea. Above him the lights of tiny villages flickered against the mountain. A slight wind whispered across the grass fields. *I see why Mama loves this place. She likes getting her breath taken away.*

Maria wanted to touch, she just knows better. I'm glad someone does. You've never been much on anticipation, have you bud? You would have crawled through that window and curled up in the crook of her body and started kissing the backs of her shoulders. And then what? You've always possessed the words before the touching but you can't come up with them after. Words are so difficult after the touching when you've only known the girl a short while and you know her heart is as fragile as yours. Some girls are satisfied with silence but not so many. Most want to hear something tangible, or better yet, a promise. A promise makes the touching worthwhile.

Somehow Will avoided the promises. The girls simply loved him and they allowed him the touching because he was Will and to be in his presence meant that life didn't feel futile. You're not just saying that because he's gone, are you bud? You're not just saying that to make it more of a tragedy. You're saying it because you've always known it. He gave everything purpose. Not catching any fish never mattered when you fished with Will. Driving back to Oxford on those countless dying evenings, the wind always a bit cool and raising goose bumps on your arms, a cold beer between your legs, Will talking about who could be up on the Square any given night. How he couldn't believe y'all didn't catch anything with a little wind out of the west and the weather perfect and dragging those spinner baits through the edges of beaver dams. "Can't believe we didn't land a few lunkers," he'd say. "That's all right. A bad day fishing is better than most things I know," he'd add. And you're right, Will, my friend, a bad day fishing with you is better than most things I know.

But we won't have any more, because Smitty and I failed you. We saw how much you'd had, how much you'd been lovin' on Mimi. But no, we wanted to ride and watch the fields pass by and sip on some more beer, not have to deal with that wheel, so we gave it to you, with the all out complete knowledge that you handle your liquor about the same as a freshman girl drinking her first whisky sour. Your departure was our fault, my friend, and now we won't have any bad fishing days anymore. They ought to send us down the river, Smitty and I. Accident my ass. Send your best friend to the other side and everybody tells you that these things happen.

You wouldn't buy all that if you were here, would you friend? You'd tell me not to bother with it. You'd say all we can do is play with the cards dealt, and that we simply got dealt a bad hand at Moon Lake that day. Well, I will say one thing: I wish you were here. Greece is right up your alley. We'd get Mr. Kappatos to let us take his fishing boat out every afternoon, then come in and drink wine at Maria's café and watch that moon spread light over the sea. Maybe Maria could find a friend and we'd both get a little lovin'. Or you could just steal

Maria from me. You've always had me there. You seemed to understand girls to the same degree they confused me.

Often days I wonder where life has taken Elsie. I wonder if she knows. I wish you'd talk to me, Will buddy, tell me what I ought to do. I've thought about getting on the horn and tracking her down, let her know what's taken place. That you're gone now. She deserves as much, close as y'all were. But then again I'd hate to ruin the image she carries of you, for I'm sure it's beautiful and young and true. She probably pictures you building a fire out on the bluff at Sardis, how you'd explain your method as you worked. Putting these little sticks low and then stacking some medium sized driftwood here, then a little teepee of oak branches with the leaves still on them, I can hear you now, my friend. That building a fire was art, that's what you'd say when finished. Lying back with a cold beer watching the flame spread through the web of wood exactly as you planned until it roared and sparked and smoked up into the Mississippi night. Or maybe she remembers the fishing trips to the farm lake in Holly Springs. Or the yard parties in the spring when we'd pull all the couches onto the front lawn. Or maybe she simply remembers what you said to her at the airport. That final day. I don't know what you said, bud, but I'm sure you said something fine. Something that made her want to turn around and head back towards Mississippi. Sometimes I miss Elsie. I think Smitty and I fell a little in love ourselves.

I hate to bother you with all this, friend, but I don't have anyone else to tell. Kefalonia is a good ways from Tupelo, and besides, Smitty's taking your departure pretty hard. Last thing he needs is to hear about my problems. And I guess they're not really problems in the true sense of the word. I simply miss my girl. Nothing unique, no complicated inner struggle. I just miss my Lily. I can't shake her. And I've always been able to shake girls. Sometimes in less than a few days. But Lily rearranged things inside me, and I don't know if I'll ever get it straightened out. Maybe this happens to folks and they simply live on, doing the best they can to suppress that remembered voice that keeps calling them home. Thing is, I'm not even sure I'd be welcome. There's a difference between missing a girl who'd receive you with open arms and missing a girl who's moved on for good. Who's an actress now, surrounded by boys with the same passion as hers, boys from up east who I don't know anything about, boys I don't know how to compete with. Maybe I was only as good as the place we were in. Even though you and I believe in no finer a town, I often wonder if Lily needed something different than Oxford. Than Mississippi. I just don't know what to buy anymore, Will.

Tell me what to believe and what to discard. It's all up in the air. I don't know whether to blame myself or blame Lily or just accept the fact that life separates people for a reason. Although I'd hate to buy that one. That one tends to imply that I don't have any say in the matter. And when it comes to Lily, I believe my voice relevant. I wish you were here, bud, and I wish we had a little cooler of cold beer. We could sit *here on this rock and listen to Greece at night, to the wind coming down off the mountain. It sounds the same as Sardis in early winter, when the geese come down on that north blow. Course there's no mountains in Mississippi. But the wind sounds the same.*

As for this Maria girl, well, I've gotten lucky, old friend. Maybe someone upstairs figured I was due for a blessing, sending it in a form I could most appreciate. Maybe you sent her to me, maybe you've got that kind of power now. I'd like to think so. She touched my arm this morning in the jeep exactly like Lily used to when riding out to Sardis in the early evening to love on each other. So, as you can imagine, it got to me. She's pretty I tell you. And her words are relevant. You can tell she lives with guts. Nothing like a strong girl developing a crush on you. It's good for the confidence, bad for the heart. The ones that don't really need you are the ones you fall for. You become a wanting, a longing. Not a necessity. When you're a necessity it's time to move on. Those girls never had a chance, did they Will? You taught me that more than anybody. When they leaned on you, you ran. When they ran from you, you followed. Why does the damn heart have to work that way? If it didn't I wouldn't have anything to write about, I guess, and we wouldn't have had anything to talk about while fishing.

I need to quit rambling and crawl up in that guest house, rest up. Looks like I'm gonna be chasing a girl while I'm here. She's chaseable, I'll tell you that right now. There's something about her, though, something I wish you were here to help me figure out. As if she knows the end before the story even gets rolling.

It's too fine out here to be alone, William. You and I could build a fire and sip on some beers all night, watching these stars and listening to that sea hit the rocks. It ain't Mississippi, bud, but it works. I'm glad I listened to Mama. She used to say that she didn't fall off the truck yesterday, and it's only now that I'm starting to believe her.

If you don't mind I'd like to do this again, every once in a blue moon. Let you know what's going on in my life, let you know if the browns are spawning up on the White River, or if the winter crappie start hitting at Walls. And the girls, I'll always tell you about the girls. I know you wouldn't accept it if you were down here, but I apologize for what happened. For taking your time away from you like that. I know you'd say it wasn't anyone's fault, but you still need to let me repent a bit. If only for my sake. I've got a hole down in my gut because I've started to realize that I'll never sit in a duck blind with you again, or drink a Maker's and water with you up at the Grocery, or ride horses out at Campbell's farm in late October when the leaves come down off the big oaks. Regardless of fault, it's hard to let go. I know you still had a ten-pound bass in you, and a few more mallard doubles in the timber. I can't help but feel I had a role in stealing that from you. Talking to you out loud helps me deal, helps me remember why we cut our palms in the Crowder goose pit that morning and became blood brothers. We didn't take it serious that morn, laughed like it was a joke. But now it means more than I can even grasp. Smitty would say I'm being silly *now. Maybe he'd be right. I don't care. I figure you dying allows me a little leeway as far as craziness goes.*

Maria

She lay awake for a good long while, staring through the half-light, wondering if he'd return and try again. *I did the right thing, there's no reason to hurry this. But I don't know if I could refuse him if he came back. We only have two weeks. Maybe that's reason not to do anything at all.*

She closed her eyes and thought about the day, so free with all the wind swirling in the jeep. The open road. The fine words they'd shared. *It's a bit strange being so indiscriminate with a boy I've only known two days. Yet natural. Maybe folks just go about this life wrong. They live their days with shields raised, protecting everything that is intimate and sincere from all who pass them by, even from their friends, family, confidants. People sharing their petty trivialities when they ought to be offering their hearts. Even on a morning car ride to Argostoli, or in the market shopping for fruit, or tending the watermelons in the garden. Why it took a black-haired boy from Mississippi for me to realize this I'll never know.*

Keane and I possessed this sacred alter of emotions between us, but I didn't realize its presence until I lost it. I thought everyone experienced such relationships, that sincerity was inherent at every step of our lives. My years in England seem almost dreamy now, as if I lived them in refusal of the greater world. It must have been those clouds, low and rushing across the sky.

She closed her eyes and saw an image of her father, in the hospital at Argostoli, what seemed like a hundred wires attached to his chest and nose and throat. During those days she had to remind herself who the man was that lay there, helpless. That it was the same man who lifted garden boulders like leaves, who worked the café from sunup to sundown. That fished the sea with his brother Spiro. That swam in the shallows with his child daughter riding upon his back. The man who provided her life had left a long time before that afternoon when the doctor removed the wires, and Maria had promised herself that day to remember only his years of strength, not this last year of confinement to a lonely, stone-colored room.

There's only one real tragedy. It's not necessarily tragic that Father died. Nor Mama's suicide. That was merely a decision which I don't possess the right to judge. What's tragic is that my father didn't see the sea at Katelios before he died, or the church at Mavrata, or the rows of olive trees in the valley of the patron saint. All the sights he knew so well. He saw a room, a wall. A lone chair and a side table in the corner, diffused light through the curtained window, the figure of a strange man in a white coat. If mercy exists, it ought to allow a soul one closing choice: what to lay its final eyes upon.

Maria sat up in bed, swallowed the tightness in her throat. Outside the window she heard a rustling in the grass.

"Cole," she said. There was no answer, and she lay down in disappointment. *I'm tired of nights alone. Silly. As if I didn't share such emotion with every living soul.*

The street lay wet from a dawn shower. The sea like oil. A dampness in the air. Maria came up the steps of the café adorning a smile. Yanni looked up from his newspaper, sipped his coffee.

"Now tell," he said.

"Tell what?" Maria said, disappearing into the kitchen to fetch a cup.

"Wherever yesterday took you."

"That was a beautiful English sentence, my cousin. As natural as a boy from Mississippi."

"You are quite confusing," Yanni said.

"I try my best."

"Please tell. Neither Thalia or I could think of guess."

"Think of a guess, Yanni. You say 'a' before 'guess'."

"A guess," Yanni said.

"That's better. I went riding with a boy from Mississippi." Yanni looked across the sea at Zachynthos.

"You enjoy doing the funny in the morning, you know. Always in the morning you do the funny."

"Yanni, my cousin. Please speak in Greek when you're not sure about the English."

"I wasn't right?"

"No."

"Well I'm sorry for my poor English. But you still have something to tell. My life, no secrets. You have the secrets."

"I told you. We went through Argostoli and took the mountain road to Fiskardo. Drank wine and watched the sailboats dock. He loved the sight of Ithaki. We returned through the interior valley. He'd never been in a convent before."

Yanni shook his head.

"Yanni, my cousin," Maria said, placing her hand upon his, "I'm not doing the funny. Remember the American couple that stays with my godparents?"

"I think."

"It's their son. He's visiting Kefalonia, staying down at the Kappatoses'. In the back house."

Yanni nodded. "And you went riding with him?"

"We're all adults here, Yanni. Don't act like my father."

"Mr. Kappatos said nothing about it?"

"Oh please. Will you ever change? As if your only duty in life was to protect me from nothing."

"Well there's no one else to do it," Yanni said. "You have no father now and it seems your godfather won't even look after you."

"If only you had his wisdom."

"Wonderful. Now we get to insults. We have no insult in quite a while. Thank you."

"Your English falters when you're mad, Yanni."

Yanni rose and went back to the kitchen, pulling pots from the cabinets, beginning the lunch preparations. Maria followed him, leaning against the wall as he ignored her. After several minutes of silence Maria asked, "Yanni, don't you think I deserve a new friend? I don't believe a new friend is too radical."

"Radical?"

"I mean out of the question."

"Out of the question?"

"Extreme, I don't think it's too extreme."

"Extreme?"

"Jesus, Yanni," Maria said, "Did you skip this chapter in your lesson book?"

Yanni ceased working, setting his knife down on the counter where he'd been chopping celery. He looked to Maria as a grin spread across his face. Maria went to him, laughing. She embraced his neck and whispered with her eyes closed, "Your concern flatters me, cousin. But I have to allow myself some freedom."

Yanni left the café during siesta. Maria dusted the framed prints hanging in the dining room. An afternoon wind rose and it swept through the café, fluttering the tablecloths. She sighed, halted her work and contemplated the refreshing distraction that Cole's arrival offered.

Mississippi, she thought. It was as intangible to her now as those first words of English over fifteen years ago. But she didn't dismiss the thought of it. Becks and England, in the very least, taught her to believe in other lands, other lives. To know that they were true, that they existed, that somewhere Delta fields of cotton ran towards a river levee. *Whatever fields of cotton look like. If Cole says that my clothes come from the dirt of the Mississippi Delta then I believe him.*

I do hope he comes. It would be quite the rejection if he didn't, for there's little else to keep his attention. Watch Nouno toil in the garden. Listen to Nouna chatting with her cousins from Argostoli on the telephone. He'll come. He wanted to take things further last night, and you dissented. Resisting a boy usually lights a fire under him. He'll come with bells on this time. A determined boy is a fine thing to behold, as long as you are the object of the determination.

Keane said he'd come to Kefalonia. You refused. What did you expect of the boy? To never touch another in agony over losing you?

You just didn't like to hear it, especially from that Scottish girl who lived on your floor. For some strange reason, she was always jealous of you. To tell you that Keane had found another made her day. And ruined yours. One spoken sentence can equal the power of a four-year love. Tear it down. You wept as you finished packing up your belongings, didn't you? You'd stayed in Durham for another month after graduation, simply to take it all in, a few final weeks of absorbing England, the river Weir, the rolling country on the train to St. Andrews with the short stone walls and fields of pure, forever green. Keane had left for London three weeks before, the day after graduation. And less than a month later, the Scottish girl said, he was dating a redhead who worked for a designer in Covent Garden. She'd heard from a classmate who saw them at a bar along the river Thames by Tower Bridge. But you couldn't blame him, could you Maria? Not after those words, so lacking the love you'd effortlessly given him for four years.

"There's no sense in any of it, Keane," you had said.

"Hell with this job in London," Keane said, "I can come to Kefalonia. I'm young. Who's making any decisions now? I've got my whole life for a career."

"I wouldn't ask you to give London up."

"Look what I'm giving up if I don't."

"I can't let you, Keane. It won't work. Everything's stacked against us."

"Why are you dead set on looking at it that way?" Keane asked. You had looked over at him, sitting in the grass by the old Durham cathedral.

"I can't deny where I'm from, Keane."

Then four years of emotion ending with the briefest and simplest of statements, spoken by this boy Keane with his mild British tone: "Denying me is the only answer I need."

He did kiss you. Twice. Once on the cheek and once on the forehead as he brushed away your hair. Then rising, and without looking back, without attempting to gain some desperate and lasting picture of his girl, he walked down the cobblestone street in front of St. Chad's College, disappearing around the corner as insignificantly as if headed to the store for a pack of cigarettes. To London. To a new life void of a Greek Maria. To a redhead the Scot said.

Cole sat on the small veranda across the street from the café. He watched three fishermen free their boat from the rocks and head out to sea. Tourist children making sand castles downbeach. In the distance a sailboat drifted along the southern shore of Kefalonia, its white mast wavering in the slight afternoon wind.

Maria spotted him after awhile. She poured a carafe of wine, fetched two tumblers and joined him. She sat and filled the glasses. Cole took one in hand, nodded, raised a silent toast and sipped. Maria laughed like a child, as if they were acting out a dramatic scene.

"I didn't know if you'd come," she said.

"The lies of a beautiful girl. It's been too long."

"I speak the truth."

"Right," Cole said, "Like I'd had my fill of you."

"I'm being silly," Maria said.

"Yes, but I like it." Cole shook his head. "This is only the third day, Maria. We act like childhood friends."

"It happens. But I'm glad you said something. I've been thinking about it this morning even. I've decided it's not strange to feel close too quickly, only uncommon."

"But isn't strange the same thing as uncommon?" Cole said.

"Strange is when the heart feels opposite what you'd expect. Like feeling sadness upon the birth of a child. Uncommon is when the heart feels as it should, but has been too long deprived of the chance."

"You should pen a book," Cole said.

"I told you, I only read. Writing is for the complicated."

"I forgot about your simplicity." Cole drank his wine and looked out across the sea at Zachynthos. Maria noticed his profile. The slender face, the black, feathery hair, cheeks reddened from yesterday's drive in the jeep. *He could pass for a Greek boy, although that Mississippi drawl gives him away.*

A crush on this boy has you back to the basics, doesn't it? We're always so vulnerable to our most basic desires. In the end, all we want is someone to lie with in the evening who we enjoy looking at and who we enjoy talking to. A simple thought for a simple desire. I want to look at you; I want to talk to you. I'd give up my years in England to forever have someone to kiss my shoulders before sleep. Look at Mother. She had that someone. And she saw no purpose without that someone. As if this decision she made, the seeming choice of all choices, wasn't even a decision at all. Like a fact. No partner, no life.

"I'm rubbing off on you," Cole said.

"How so?"

"You just left me for awhile."

"It's the sea's fault," Maria said, "It makes me dreamy."

"Rightly so."

"Did you sleep well?"

"Yes," he said, "Although sleep's never been a problem for me. I'm more tormented during the daylight hours."

"Oh, you're missing out," Maria said, "It's glorious to lie in bed for hours on end, the ceiling your only comfort."

"And what does a pretty girl like you have to lose sleep over?" Cole said. Maria looked away, as if hearing a distant sound. "I'm sorry," he said, "I wasn't thinking. It slipped my mind."

"It's nothing," she said, touching the inside of his forearm. "We get all of life. Not just the parts we prefer." Cole raised his glass and she chimed hers against it.

"To life, that unprejudiced son of a bitch," he said.

"Can you swim in those shorts?" Maria asked.

"Every day of the week."

"Come," she said, "I'll show you where I spent most of my childhood."

They walked along the main street of Katelios, Maria catching glances from all the curious merchants, waving when she caught their eyes.

"We'll be the talk of the village," she whispered to Cole.

Along the beach with its rocky sand, the sea washing up at their feet. Tourists smiled at them, offering salutations. One lady spoke in German and Maria nodded in return. The beach gave way to boulders worn smooth by time, by water. Maria led Cole on a narrow pathway between the rocks, reaching behind to hold his hand on several tight ledges. She had removed her sandals, holding them in her free hand.

"If you took your shoes off it would be easier," she said.

Cole watched his feet. "I'm trying to concentrate, leave me alone." Below, the sea lay clear. The water's surface like clean glass.

"We're almost there," she said. They crossed another ledge, down a grassy path. Then upon a wide, flat boulder that hung twenty feet above the sea, its surface smooth as old marble. Looking back from where they'd walked, Cole saw Katelios, the stores and newsstands, the colorful bathing suits of the tourists on the beach. Maria's café.

"Well," she said.

"I wish we had a cooler of beer," Cole said.

"We can come back sometime. Better prepared."

"Will would have loved this place."

"You should have brought this friend of yours," Maria said, "I have cousins."

"Yeah," he said. "Maybe next time." He removed his shirt and shoes, walked over to the edge of the boulder. "How deep is it?"

"Deep enough to dive."

"Promise?"

"Promise."

Cole jumped, allowing his body to rotate over itself on the way down, entering the sea with hands outstretched, already swimming as he entered. Coming up for air, shaking the water from his eyes, turning back towards the rock where Maria stood removing her clothes. Underneath she wore her bathing suit.

"You knew that you'd bring me here."

"So?"

"At the café you said you didn't know whether I'd come or not."

"So I was lying."

"Am I being that obvious?"

"All boys are obvious," she said, "But yes, you're not exactly confusing me." Cole went underwater, swimming freely, coming up for a moment's worth of air then under again.

Maria dove, the water fresh and clean on her skin, memories of childhood entering her mind with the first feeling of wetness and sea. She swam out to Cole where he was treading water in place, staring at the outline of Zachynthos.

"It's always there, isn't it?" Maria said.

"It's so mythic. I mean, that's the only word for it. An island mountain rising up out of the water like that, with all the sea-haze surrounding it."

"Guess what?" Maria said.

"What?"

"Kefalonia looks just like that when standing on Zachynthos."

"It does?"

"They all do.   Everything depends on your viewpoint, southern boy."

"What a literature major you are."

"And what did you study?" she said, the cold water making her shiver a bit.

"The same."

"Criticizing your own people?"

"No," he said, "But we do need to laugh at ourselves as much as possible.   We're not exactly a stable lot."

"I'll agree with that," Maria said. "Listen, don't worry about being obvious. You evoke plenty of mystery in other areas."

"Thanks for the pity."

"It's not pity. No girl likes a boy to be mysterious in how he feels towards her. Just in other ways."

"Okay, I'm embarrassed now," he said, going under, swimming up behind Maria, taking her legs, pulling her down with him. She yelled as they went down, reaching for him, grabbing his arms and pulling him up. They came up out of the water in half embrace, and when they opened their eyes their mouths were little more than a few inches apart. Maria watched the water roll down Cole's face, the pure blackness of his hair. Cole dropped his eyes and released her. He floated on his back as he began to talk.

"I'm a bit jealous," he said.

"Of what?"

"Of you getting to live this life, in this place."

"Listen to you.   Is that an admission that Mississippi has competition?"

"No."

"Sounded so."

"It's too different, Maria. You can't compare a book to a song."

"Who's being the literature major now?"

"I'm serious. Mississippi is mud and woods and geese coming down the river in winter. Kefalonia is rock and olive trees and a blue sea."

"I'd like to go to Mississippi," Maria said. Cole splashed his hand in the water.

"It's not like this. It's not breathtaking to look at. But it has ghosts and blood and soul."

"Speak English, boy."

"I'm trying to," he said, "Nobody knows how to describe Mississippi. Most folks who only come for a visit don't see anything special about it. And I understand that. It's the kind of land you have to share a decade with to even begin to understand."

"I thought you grew up in Memphis?"

"Memphis. Mississippi. Same difference. Memphis starts the Delta so it's different than Tennessee in a lot of ways. Tennessee's known for its hills and mountains in the east. The Delta's flat as a board. Cotton. Beans. Besides, I spent every weekend in Mississippi. My old man's hunting camp, inside the levee. You've never seen woods like that in your life, Maria."

"Your voice," Maria said, "It changes when you talk about Mississippi. Like you're talking about someone you know."

"I'm a little silly about land. I don't know a lot of places like my folks. But I do know that I can hunt that tract inside the levee with a blindfold on. My old man's belonged to the camp all his life; his father before him. And I know it twice as good. When we hunt together I tell him where to go."

"I don't understand most of this," Maria said, "But it's nice to listen to."

"I'm boring you."

"You're not," Maria said, "But this swimming is making me hungry. Let's go to the café and eat something."

Back at the café Maria brought out a bowl of Greek salad, a loaf of fresh bread, a saucer of tzaziki. Cole ran pieces of bread through the tzaziki. Maria stuck tomatoes with her fork and watched him.

"Did you not eat anything this morning?" she asked.

"Your godmother was already in the garden when I woke. I didn't want to send her back to the kitchen."

"How's the bread?"

"Good as a government check."

"Come again?" Maria said.

"You remember, one of the sayings from yesterday. You'll learn 'em. Just give it time."

Maria poured two tumblers of wine and they walked out to the beach. They sat in the sand and sipped the cold wine. The day still, the sun more than half-way through its recurring task.

"Maria?"

"Cole?"

"How long have they been gone?" Maria lowered her chin, squinted into the lowering white sun. She drank, wiped her lips with the back of her hand.

"A few months."

"You seem to be doing well."

"Yes. Seems that way. Your distraction helps."

"Have you done this well since?"

"Sticking to our trend of no small talk, huh?"

"You don't have to answer," Cole said, "Just tell me to be quiet."

"No. It's fine." she said. Maria set her empty glass in the sand. "For about a month I did so terribly that I didn't know if I was going to make it. I think I went three days without a wink of sleep during one week. I didn't know one could feel so isolated, even from my aunts and uncles, cousins. Those who loved me. I felt like it was me versus this encompassing conspiracy of sadness that everyone else knew how to overcome. I felt weak. I lost the ability to enjoy the simplest things. Lunch, an afternoon nap, swimming. If it wasn't for my parents' garden they might have put me in the hospital."

"The garden?"

"I spent hours upon hours weeding, watering, fertilizing. I made myself believe that my existence depended upon the success of the garden. As if the tomatoes were my children; the Japanese plums my grandchildren. It gave me enough purpose to ward off complete sickness."

"I take my folks for granted," Cole said.

"Are you close with them?"

"To an extent. It's kind of strange, though. My folks are really into each other. They're still in love like high schoolers. And that's great and all, no doubt. I'm happy for them. Thing is, they don't really need me to be happy. I don't know. Hard to explain. It's like they do their own thing and I do my own thing and we're completely civil to each other when we cross paths. I think Mama realizes this and it makes her sad.

"School made it worse. Our communication broke down 'cause I spent all breaks and holidays hunting and fishing with my boys in Mississippi. I wasn't the kind to go home and sit by the fire and tell my parents all the wonderful experiences of the semester. We never exchange cross words, there's just this formal stiffness in our relationship. Maybe it's good. I know a lot of friends who are too close to their folks, parents always trying to run the kids' lives because they feel so involved."

"You almost sound comfortable telling me all this," Maria said.

"What do you mean?"

"Your voice has been hesitant up until now."

"C'mon."

"I'm serious. Sure we had a lovely time yesterday driving to Fiskardo, but there was hesitation in your words the whole day."

"How can you tell?"

"I just can," she said.

"What do you mean, 'hesitation'?"

Maria took a sip of wine. The wind rose warm on her face. She cupped a handful of sand and allowed it to sift through her fingers.

"Like you were hiding something," she said. Cole leaned back upon the sand and stared at the sky. He listened to the laughing sounds of tourist children downbeach, two fishermen rigging tackle on their boat. The bark of a stray dog on the main street of the village.

"I'm just shy," Cole said.

Maria shook her head. "You boys are extremely talented at dodging questions."

"Hold on, you're not gonna throw me in that boy category are you?" he said, grabbing her ribs.

"Oh, stop it," Maria said, "I'm ticklish."

"Good to know."

"See. See what I mean. I was one inch from getting you to say something relevant, and you've gone and completely changed the mood."

"I'm a veteran," Cole said.

"You're a boy," Maria said, "Nothing more, nothing less."

"All I've ever been."

Out of the corner of her eye Maria saw Yanni walking down the street, headed back to the café from his nap. She grabbed Cole's arm, pulled him to his feet.

"Come. I want you to meet my cousin Yanni. We run the café together. Don't mention anything about trying to sneak in my window last night. He'd probably try to hurt you."

"I know what to say. You think it's the first time I tried to sneak in a girl's window."

They entered the café as Yanni examined the meat in the freezer. He looked to Maria and Cole, then back to the freezer quickly as if not seeing them.

"Yanni, this is the boy I spoke of. Cole Morgan." Yanni shut the freezer and approached them. He extended his hand to Cole without meeting his eye.

"Good to see you," Cole said.

"Yes," Yanni said, "Maria, have you any ideas for supper?"

"Whatever you like. You're the chief."

"Chief?" Yanni said.

"Decision maker."

"Okay then." Yanni nodded to Cole and returned to the kitchen. Maria rolled her eyes and led Cole out to the street.

"You're a glorious swimmer and we must swim again."

"Affirmed," he said.

"I must tend to my earthly duties now."

"I understand." Cole winked and, without saying more, departed down the main street. Maria watched him until he disappeared around the corner past the newsstand. She thought of the moment they'd risen out of the water together, the wetness of Cole's lips so present, his black hair falling across his eyes, droplets of sea running down his face. An image to keep.

Maria sliced tomatoes and cucumbers and onions for the evening salad. Yanni thawed the meat and preheated the ovens and remained silent throughout his work. Maria occasionally glanced up to see if he would make eye contact with her. He would not. He labored as if alone. Maria stood it for half an hour then said: "I don't need you to look out for me."

"Nobody else will," Yanni said.

"Oh please. Would you stop with all that. You act as if Cole was some criminal. It's so absurd."

"He's not Greek, Maria."

"Neither are most of the tourists we serve."

"They do not try to take advantage of you."

"Yanni, the last time I checked, there existed no laws against Greek girls spending time with American boys."

"No matter. The boy takes advantage of you. I can tell. I know."

"Why? Could you explain why? Because he's not from Kefalonia? I never thought you'd fall victim to such ignorance, Yanni, I really didn't."

Yanni dropped a pan of cold prawns. They scattered on the floor. Maria placed her face within her hands. "You handle supper if you're so wise," she said.

Outside the last crimson light dropped below the western sea. Maria walked to the spot where she and Cole had sat drinking wine. She sat Indian style in the sand. Zachynthos appeared through the dusk, the lights of distant villages beginning to shine like fireflies. *It's such an arbitrary thing to get upset about. A boy and a girl being wonderful to each other. Where does Yanni find fault in that? I'll tell you where he finds fault. He finds fault in the boy being from another country. If this was the Sami boy everyone would be dancing around in celebration. But because Cole came from some distant place he somehow poses a threat. The finest thing I learned while living away was the similarities of our most basic desires, no matter the place we originate from. Keane wanted the same thing Cole wants. I probably want the same thing this Lily girl wanted.*

Not as if I need Yanni's permission. I'll do what pleases my heart, especially now, when my heart deserves sincere attention and more. But it would be nice to have a blessing. I often act as if I'm above the need for a family's blessing, but it is there, present and painful, somewhere in my soul, a place we have no name for. Just look at what I did to Keane. Broke his heart for the sake of parents who didn't live another year. Maybe you could get Keane back. Stop it Maria. Go help Yanni. He can't cook and serve no matter how wise and noble he believes himself.

Cole

Cole ate a late supper of greens and tomatoes and baked fish with several glasses of homemade wine. Mrs. Kappatos asked about his mother, how things were going in Memphis. It took a long while to say very little with Mrs. Kappatos, for her English had to be taken slowly, with explanation. Mr. Kappatos spoke of Cole's father again, hinting at the sincerity of the friendship in spite of the distance and language barriers. He shook his head and grinned, recounting how they'd met so long ago, down at the café.

"I served in Greek navy and learned little English. Me and you father read paper at café and start to talk. Keep talk since."

They talked more fishing and the old man confirmed that he'd take Cole on the sea in the next few days. They nibbled on cookies for dessert and drank another glass of wine. Cole said his thanks and retired to the guest house.

He rested on his back, thinking about his parents' friendship with the Kappatoses. To have met so young, so far from home. *I can't imagine why they'd stay in touch that long. Sure you can, bud. The property deals. Your old man keeps the friends that make him money. Why here, though? Why did my folks come to Kefalonia among all the other islands? Why did they begin this process that has ultimately led me to Maria, by way of losing Will? It's all a bit much, especially after several glasses of the wine. The wine makes you* believe that everything bears significance when our lives are nothing more than a random succession of events that we translate into fate at our own discretion. Your parents took a trip when they were young, met a couple their age, remained friends, allowed you to see another country by way of this friendship. But you have to bring in Maria and Will, don't you old boy, as if there's something to figure out in the midst of all this pain and possible love. It's simply life. So one of the players has dark hair and olive skin and touches your forearm just as Lily did, and when you rise up out of the sea in her arms and the water runs down her chest into the folds of her bathing suit it's possible to believe that you've found a new partner. But it's just life, and it's going on in Mississippi too, even while you're gone. They just don't have the good wine.

You need to start writing all these unanswerable questions. They're no good for the thoughts but they're all right on paper. And don't forget about the old man. You owe him. You ought to write a story for every time he took you fishing. You should write the time in Louisiana when y'all arrived in the evening and went down to the restaurant in Cypress Cove and ate cold shrimp and raw oysters and the rain came hard and steady against the window and y'all had to drive so slow through the storm back over to Venice Marina. How it was blowing. How y'all went to sleep so quickly on the houseboat because of the long drive from Memphis and the oysters and the cold beer. Waking in the middle of the night to make water and seeing the trash cans blowing past the window like sheets of paper. Looking out,

seeing the five-foot white caps in the marina, hollering at the old man.
"What, what, was I snoring," he asked. "No," you said, "It's a damn
blow. The real thing." How he walked over to the window and saw
two fishing boats capsized and the rods blowing across the wooden
docks. "Well," he said, scratching his head, "This rig has pontoons
built under two feet of concrete. Safest place to be in all of Louisiana
right now. If it takes us well then it takes us. If we go, New Orleans
will go too. I'd rather go in my sleep."

He went back over to his bunk and began to breathe the steady
rhythm of rest a few minutes later, but you watched the storm for two
hours. It was so hatefully beautiful. You couldn't let it go and you told
yourself that night you'd write it but you haven't yet, huh old boy? It's
easy to remember all the things that need to be written, but writing
them, well, that's another matter in itself. You always have an excuse
for not putting it all to paper, whether it be the crappie biting at North
Lake or new mallards working the timber in west Tennessee or the
browns spawning below the dam on the Little Red.

Now you've got this boy lost in the timber and you can't decide
what to do with him. You can't leave him standing in that backwater
in early January when the sun drops before five. Especially if he's got
a leak in his waders. He doesn't have a prayer if his feet get wet.
Finish this boy's story before you leave Kefalonia.

He rose and walked over to the open window. It was clear and
the lights of Zachynthos villages hung eye-level, stars not of the

heavens. A mild wind rose and fluttered the sage grasses up on the mountain. The sea black, ever present. Cole shook his head. *That river back home gives me enough trouble, I wonder what growing up by the sea would have done to me. I'll give it one thing, it was good as gold to Maria and I this afternoon. Her skin. The water beading across the backs of her shoulders. She even makes Will go away for a little while and I don't even think the old boy would mind. He'd probably be proud, to forget him on account of a girl. Especially one like this, who listens as if you're the only one who's ever said a relevant word to her. But you know that's not true. You know this Keane fellow was pretty sharp for her to give him time, but it's still nice to imagine that you hung her moon. Lily never said it but that's why she left. Her moon hung over a northern sky illuminated by the lights of theatres. Your moon kept watch over Delta cotton fields and oxbow river lakes. Maybe Maria's moon is a little more akin to yours. It sure would be nice. You could wake to that face every morning, couldn't you old boy? Course you said that a few days ago at the barbecue place in New Albany. That's all right. Nobody ever said there's only one. Well they did but they were dead wrong.*

Cole hesitated for an hour, sitting on the edge of the bed, blue jeans and boots on. Then he reminded himself that he had nine days left in Kefalonia. That he was young. That Maria lived alone in a house on the southern shore of an island in the middle of the Ionian Sea. That people worked day jobs in offices that they hated and dreamed of places and girls that looked like this land and this girl before him now. He crossed the fields just back of the village, then past the newsstand and down the quiet, empty side street. Her window was open, a faint light shining from within. He watched her read under the lamplight, the way she turned the pages, the way her black reading specs sat halfway down her nose like those of a professor.

"I've come to bother you again."

Maria glanced up. "Could you please come back another time, I'm reading Joyce."

"I'll save you some time," Cole said, "Wet Irish streets and emotionally rough men. Eternally troubled people without a hope of redemption."

"What if someone does that with your life's work one day?" Maria said, "Reduces it into two sentences to impress a girl?"

"I'll be proud if they can come up with two sentences," Cole said, leaning both elbows on the windowsill.

"Come in."

He crawled through the window and sat on the floor, back leaned against the wall. The covers were pulled up over Maria's legs, the upper part of her spaghetti strap nightgown showing.

An image of Lily entered Cole's thoughts, how she used to lie on the bed while he sat on the floor reading his stories aloud. How when he finished she'd lay there a minute longer in silence, then ask him why he never wrote about her. *Why write about girls when you have fishing and grandfathers, you'd say, sarcastically, avoiding the substance of the question. But you wrote about her all right, you just never offered those pieces aloud. They possessed a little more of yourself than you were willing to share.*

"You seem very natural at this," Maria said, "Sneaking in a girl's window."

"I've had my practice."

"I should take Yanni's advice and run from you."

"Why does your cousin not like me?" Cole asked.

"Because you're a boy and American."

"I thought those were positive traits."

"If you're a Mississippi girl they are, but if you're a Kefalonian orphan with overbearing cousins they're not."

Cole noticed a picture on her night table: an older couple standing on the beach at Katelios in front of an old fishing boat. The mother resembled a short Maria and the father bore dark skin and black, curly hair, no shirt, thin but tone muscles in his arms.

"Fine picture, huh?" Maria said.

"Yes."

"You don't need many pictures," Maria said, "Everybody thinks we should have albums and albums of photos that exhibit our life and family and accomplishments. A few is really all one needs. Just to show who raised us and that we were all happy for a little while."

"I agree," Cole said.

"When I was little," Maria explained, leaning back against her pillow, "I always thought I'd marry a Greek man like Papa and he'd take over the café and I'd go fishing with him in the early mornings. That we'd have seven kids and they would run through the streets free as stray dogs."

"It could still happen," Cole said.

"I know too much now."

"About Greek men?"

"No, about how it all turns out. It never turns out as you imagine."

"I'd still say the odds of you marrying Greek are pretty good," Cole said.

"Yes, but it'll be different. As a child your folks appear like a brother and a sister. You don't see all the complications of romance because your heart's not to that level yet."

"I'm never gonna do it," Cole said.

"You will, friend. You enjoy the company of girls too much not to fall victim."

"Well," he said, "Let's just say I won't settle because my friend lonesome visits me. I'd rather be lonesome and just have an old golden retriever to sleep at the foot of my bed than to settle."

"Agreed."

Cole pulled his knees to his chest. *How we end up places. Our friendship is merely days old, and yet, I haven't felt this close to anyone since Lily left. Even to Smitty. He's been too torn up about Will to deal with anyone else's thoughts.*

"Who are you and where am I?" Cole asked.

"I'm Maria and you're in Katelios."

"Is that how it works?"

"That's how it works," Maria said.

"It's that simple?"

"It's that simple," she said.

"Why do we make things complex that are simple?"

"Because we read a few books."

"So you wouldn't suggest studying literature to anyone else?" Cole asked.

"Not unless you are rich and single. If you're rich and single you can read the books and go to the cafés in London and talk about them to other rich and single people forever and always and life will be dramatic and lovely. But if you have to go to work or you're in love for real or your parents die then the books aren't so great."

"Now you're speaking my language," Cole said.

"Yes, I know, because you're rich and single," Maria said.

"No."

"Then what? You don't work and your folks are alive. Are you in love for real?"

"Possibly," Cole said.

"Go to your guest house, southern boy."

"Are you serious?"

"Yes."

"Why?" he said.

"Because we have a big day tomorrow. We go to my name-day party at the little church above the village Pastra. All afternoon. You must be rested. Plus, if you stay any longer you'll probably say something you'll regret in the morning."

"I've done it all my life," Cole said, "Why stop now?"

"Because you're in Kefalonia now and they aren't very kind to American boys who play with girls' hearts."

"I'll accept that as a threat," Cole said. "What's name-day?"

"You'll find out tomorrow."

"Maria?"

"Yes."

"My friend Will. The one I've been talking about."

"Yes?"

"I lost him beginning of the summer."

"Lost him? Like I lost my parents?"

"Yes," Cole said.

"Do you want to talk about it now or some afternoon out on the rocks?"

"Some afternoon out on the rocks," he said.

They rode slowly up the mountain to Mavrata, Mr. Kappatos pointing out different houses, cousins and friends who lived in each. Part of the early morning sun peeked over the mountain, the distant sea drenched in its light. Dew lay on the sage grasses and grape vines. Wildflowers strewn upon the mountainside, the air cool, like October mornings in Mississippi. Both Mr. Kappatos and Cole shirtless, arms hanging from the window, going to work with hands upon soil, upon earth. The only task all were meant for.

Mr. Kappatos turned down the narrow street leading into Mavrata, waving to an old lady upon her patio. The houses built similar to Katelios, to Athens, to all of this Greece Cole had seen thus far. White stone, red roofing. Cole appreciated the common identity of the structures. It hinted at the unity of the people. *We are of one land.* The simplicity of the houses negating any pretense; any concern for size, for show. Only a residence, a shelter, containing the elements necessary for a home. The sincerity of the villages exhibiting the satisfaction in which the people accept their days.

Just past the village Mr. Kappatos halted the jeep. They shouldered the tools and eased across a stone wall, making their way down a narrow pathway bordered by flowers and knee-high grasses. In the unknown distance Cole heard the bells of a goat herd, the muffled calls of the herder fading into the wind.

The garden lay on high ground, upon which Cole could look down and watch the blue sea turn to foam as it met the shoreline rocks. Behind them the mountain Ainos rose sharply into the encompassing sky, while below the valley sparkled in the morning dew, more rows of olive trees and grape vines etched out of the fields of grasses and stone. Mr. Kappatos showed Cole an area of the garden that needed weeding, and Cole took to his knees with the hand-hoe, removing the random grasses from the rows of field peas, fighting the urge to only sit there and stare out at the sea and the outline of Zachynthos which rose so true and enduring upon the horizon. Mr. Kappatos hummed as he tore ripe beans from the stalk.

After a while the old man said: "You father, what he do like this? What he do outside?"

"Um, he likes to hunt some." Cole imitated holding a rifle.

"You hunt?"

"All the time," Cole answered.

"What?"

"Birds, sir. Ducks, doves, turkeys. I'll sit in a deer stand every now and then." Mr. Kappatos cocked his head. "Deer sometimes," Cole repeated.

"Me only fish," Mr. Kappatos said.

"I'll fish 'til I fall out on the ground," Cole said. Mr. Kappatos rose up and stared at the boy, confused. *You're not talking to Smitty,* *bud.* "I like to fish better than hunt," he said. Mr. Kappatos nodded, went back to picking beans.

"Your father, me. We good friends. Funny, huh."

"Yes," Cole said. "But good. So many years. To stay in touch and keep talking all that time."

"We have good time when you father and you mother come to Kefalonia. They should come more."

"And bring me with them."

"Who said you leave? No one say you leave."

Cole shrugged his shoulders. *Do I possess such courage? To* *change homes? Or is it even courage? Possibly just a decision. No, it's* *more than a decision. Especially for you. Those woods inside the levee* *are part of your blood. It would take something powerful to leave those* *acres of hardwood timber. Yet it's more than the hunting camp, huh old* *bud? It's the way the girls say your name up at the Grocery on* *Thursday afternoons in the spring when the new warmth spreads over* *the south, how they draw out their syllables, how they always preface* *your name with why.* "Why Cole Morgan, I thought we were friends." *Or the way Smitty always waited on you after class, sitting on the* *tailgate of his truck, your rods and tackle box already fetched, a cooler* *of cold beer waiting patiently on the floorboard of the truck. The way* *the fields flood in winter, covered with mallard greenheads and snow* *geese and specklebellies and teal. The way old men wave at you from* their trucks when you pass them on country roads out by Sardis Lake, raising two fingers off the steering wheel in automatic and complete friendship because you're also in a truck on the back roads of the state of Mississippi and you probably know about select cut timber and beaver dams and how much rain it takes the Tallahatchie River to flood in early November. Elsie had it right. Nothing erases where you're from.

"Cole. Come and open beans."

He walked over to where Mr. Kappatos sat on a bucket shelling beans. He sat in the soil and began to help. They worked in silence a good long while and Cole enjoyed the satisfaction of a simple task, thoughtless labor. The morning sun sat high above the mountain now, the day white and warm without a cloud to be seen in any sky.

"Maria's name-day?" Cole said.

"Yes, today."

"Will you and Mrs. Kappatos go?"

"Yes. You go?"

"Yes," Cole said, "She invited me."

"Good," Mr. Kappatos said. "There will be the music and the food and the wine."

"Sounds good."

"Cole?" Mr. Kappatos said.

"Yessir?"

"You must be careful with the girl. You understand?"

"I believe so."

"This is Kefalonia. Be friends yes. Go ride in jeep yes. Just be careful."

"Yessir."

"Especially at name-day. Don't, don't be girl's um, don't be girl's friend at name-day. Some of the people, they no understand. You see."

"I see," Cole said. "Mr. Kappatos, if you and Mrs. Kappatos don't want me to..."

"Cole. You and Maria, we understand. No problem." Mr. Kappatos pointed across the landscape. "Some people. They no understand. But some people don't matter. You see. This some people will be at name-day. They would, they would talk about nothing. Don't be with girl at name-day and they don't talk. All good, see."

"Perfectly," Cole said.

They finished shelling the beans. Mr. Kappatos led Cole through the garden, identifying the contents of each row. Patches of wildflowers grew along the edges of the toiled dirt, and Mr. Kappatos picked a certain crimson one, explaining how they crushed it to make ink dye. Cole nodded to the information, noticing Mr. Kappatos' happiness to be communicating in his broken English.

"You stay Cole. I have surprise." Mr. Kappatos disappeared down the narrow path back to the jeep. Cole waited, staring out over the sea, white caps appearing out of the deep when the wind rose. *I could do it, I could live here. But only for a girl that touches my arm as Maria does. It's all in how they reach for your arm, how they hold you above the elbow on long walks back to the car in downtown Memphis, or across the beach at Sardis Lake. They hold you above the elbow when they love you. Holding hands means as little as a kiss on the cheek. When they take your arm above the elbow for the first time, well then, you know it's going to get complicated. But it has to get complicated if you want a Lily. Or a Maria. Yes, I believe you can say that now, old bud. With little doubt if any.*

Mr. Kappatos returned with a flask of wine and two tumblers. They sat on the old, crumbling stone wall and Mr. Kappatos filled the glasses. The wine clean, cool.

Mr. Kappatos motioned across the expanse of sea. "Wine and sea in morning, good." He raised his glass. Cole chimed his against it. They finished the flask rather quickly, in silence, Cole realizing that he hadn't thought about Will since waking. *I knew this would happen. We get over our tragedies a bit too easily. Our hearts may be less compassionate than we'd like to think of them. Kefalonia has helped, no doubt, Mama was right. She knows what travel does to the mind. It makes everything, even the loss of a best friend of youth, seem less significant. In all the vastness of seas and*

countries our life becomes smaller before our eyes, and though hum-
bling, it allows for increased pleasure in the smaller experiences, such
as drinking wine with an older friend outside the village of Mavrata on
an island in the midst of the Ionian.

But you can't use it as an excuse, bud. You can't use your relative
insignificance to the world at large for an excuse to stop feeling, to stop
writing. Sure, most folks won't ever read the stories about your grandfather hunting greenhead mallards in the flooded timber in Haywood
County, Tennessee, and most won't care, but that doesn't relieve you of
the duty. You owe him to write about that afternoon hunt by Cypress Hole
when the bottom fell out of the sky, how the drakes were coming down in
the rain, breaking branches off the oaks as they lit, the backwaters rising
in the storm until they spilled over the brim of your waders and it was
almost dark and bitter cold and the old man said, "All right, let's call it
a day." And the boat ride back to camp was so cold and the rain came
harder and you couldn't figure out why it wasn't snowing. But it had
been a glorious shoot and the floor of the boat was covered in greenhead mallards and when y'all got back to the camp you breasted the
drakes on the porch and sliced the meat thin and battered it and fried
it in the skillet and cooked eggs and bacon and had breakfast for
supper. You owe the old man to write that one.

And keep writing about Will, no matter how despairing. In a few
years you'll probably write without mention of his death and folks will
ask, "Where is this friend of yours that you write so fondly about?"

And you'll make up some lie because you won't want to speak of it anymore. Except with Smitty. And Lily if she showed up on your porch one afternoon. But we don't have to worry about that, do we old bud? A Bostonian she is now. It's time to start leaving her out of your thoughts.

"Come on Cole," Mr. Kappatos said, "The tools." Cole fetched the tools and shouldered a shovel. They walked to the jeep and started back on the road to Katelios. In Mavrata women worked their flower beds and Mr. Kappatos honked as he passed. The women rose up slowly. By the time they waved they couldn't even see who it had been.

Cole sat in the sun with his pant legs pulled up to his knees.
A paper cup of wine in hand. The band played perfectly and true
while folks danced in a circle with small children leading the
movements. He watched Maria through the crowd as she
embraced and chatted with her cousins. She wore all black and
her clothes matched her hair in some unexplainable and striking
way. Cole behaved and kept away from her as Mr. Kappatos had
instructed him. *But I'm not behaving in my thoughts. I would use the*
words lovely and beautiful but they don't help in trying to explain how
she looks, now, on this day on top of this mountain by this little
Orthodox church where children dance and sing in celebration of names.

Down in the valley Cole could see the red roofs of Mavrata,
farther downbeach those of Katelios. And of course the sea.
Surrounding the mountain, surrounding existence.

The road leading up to the church had been little more than
a rocky trail, and Cole wondered about the church's history, how
the men who built it managed the stone to such an elevation. It
was small, one-room; the same grey stone both inside and out.
Cole had peered in when they first arrived at the party. A wood-
en altar in front, random icons on a table in the rear. Children
played what looked like a form of marbles on the smooth floor.

Now the sun all warm on his face, tapping his foot in the dust in rhythm to the music. He watched her and drank his wine and thought about trying to explain such an afternoon to Smitty, or to anyone back home. His parents would nod and understand, for they had been here, seen the festivities. *It takes this to understand. To listen to these children speak a different language as carefree and thoughtless as you once spoke your own. To understand the vastness of this life. To stop looking for an answer. To accept what is before you, what you hear, what you taste; so that on some distant day when your life has run its course and a young boy asks you what it's all about, you simply say, "In middle summer there's a name-day party in Kefalonia, Greece, where the band plays all afternoon and the wine goes down like water. In Mississippi autumn the deer come out from the woods in the cool early evenings of late October and they freeze in your headlights as you ride drinking beer with a friend on the country roads out by Sardis Lake; and in Tennessee winter the mallards move up the river bottoms working the green timber. When the backwaters freeze over you always try to find a little creek with some current that has kept the water open and sure enough, boy, you'll get the mallards coming in there. And in the spring, well, the spring belongs to the girls in Oxford on Thursday afternoons at the Grocery as they drink their whiskey-sours and bare their arms in spaghetti strap tops for the first time of the new year." And the boy will say, "That doesn't really answer my question," and you'll return with, "Well, son, it's all any boy ever gets for an answer."*

After awhile the men brought out platters of goat meat from the grills. Cole placed the meat between slices of bread, like a southern sandwich. Hardly anyone spoke English, so Cole returned to his chair in the sun, taking in the scene. *Conversation is unnecessary in a place like this, with people like this. Give me some food and music and a sip of wine and I'm content. And the sight of that Maria being such a patient hostess. The sincerity of her smile; I don't believe I've ever seen the likes of it before. Maybe I saw it on Lily when we were good, but that's fading now. I can feel it. Fading like the echoing calls of snow geese headed south, to places of warmth where the fields aren't frozen.*

Mr. Kappatos pulled up a chair. They spoke of fishing again, deciding to go out the next day at dawn. Mr. Kappatos specifically explained some of the land deals he'd completed with Cole's father, both in Argostoli and Sami. How funny it seemed for a lifetime of business and friendship to begin so simply reading newspapers over coffee at a café. Cole nodded, reminding himself that if it hadn't been for that meeting, he would have never met Maria. It caused him more interest in the conversation than he otherwise would have possessed. They laughed about drinking wine earlier that morning in the garden, then Mr. Kappatos invited Cole to dance with the crowd, leading him to the circle and placing him between two small girls who took his hand and showed him the steps, no way for these children to know that he hailed from a land they had never seen, save the strange tone of his voice.

Cole appreciated the kindness of the two girls. They didn't show him the steps because they accepted him. The little girls showed him the steps simply because he didn't know them. Because he was a stranger that needed help. Instruction. At one point he caught Maria watching him as she talked to a group of old women across the crowd. She didn't look away when Cole smiled.

Maria didn't send him back to the guest house that night. She whispered him through the window, the room grey from the half-moonlight enveloping the island. She took his hand, pulling him under her blanket, turning her back to him and wrapping his arm around her shoulders. There was no kiss. Cole slept soundly from the wine and sun, his face hidden under the lengths of Maria's hair. She woke him at dawn, whispering, "I suggest you not miss this fishing trip. I'd hate for the old man to come looking for you." Cole nodded, kissed the back of Maria's hand. He slipped through the window, down the side street, across the grassy field to the guest house. A light shone in the kitchen of the main house, and Cole could see Mr. Kappatos' silhouette moving about the room. Preparing to fish.

Maria

In the mild early morning before the sun cleared the mountain Ainos, Maria weeded the rows of her garden. She watered tomatoes, watermelons. She sprayed the dirt from her patio. Life still, save the meandering sound of the bread truck's bell. *You did well last night. You wanted him to stay, to hold you, but you weren't sure about going any further. Remember, only days separate you from his departure. Making love would only set you up for a fall. Yet it was nice rolling over into his warm spot this morning, at dawn, as he left. It's good to have the sheets smell like a boy again. I remember on Saturday mornings in Durham when Keane would rise early for crew practice, how I'd roll over and bury my face in his pillow.*

She showered and dressed and walked down to the café where Yanni sat drinking coffee. She fetched a cup and joined him, speaking of the menu, how the crowds seemed to be getting larger. They planned the meals for the coming days, spoke of cousins, family news. Yanni was the closest thing she'd ever had to a sibling, and in spite of his overbearing tendency, Maria loved him as much as anyone on the island. Before her parents' departure, Yanni was simply another cousin; now, it seemed, a brother. She kissed the sides of his face and said she'd be back before lunch.

She found Becks upon her patio, as always. Her old teacher nodded, smiled. Maria passed through the gate and Becks rose,

the two embracing each other sincerely, as if they'd been separated for years.

"Well," Becks said, "Did my little speech help the other day?"

"Yes," Maria said, "Your speech and a boy from Mississippi."

"You'll have to repeat that one."

"Do you remember the American couple who stays with my
godparents every few years?"

"Why yes," Becks said, "The Tennessee folks. Pleasant people."

"It's their son. He's been here several days. We've become
quite close friends I'd say."

"Well then what's this talk of Mississippi?" Becks said.

"He went to school in Mississippi, still lives there. By the way
he talks you'd think he founded the state himself."

"Sounds like an interesting chap. I'd like to meet him if I
could be so lucky."

"I'm sure it could be arranged."

"Could I get a name?" Becks asked.

"Cole. Cole Morgan."

"Simple. I like that."

"And you, professor?" Maria said.

"Well, Anatole and I went to Argostoli for supper last night.
Walked the docks. Pleasant evening. Besides that, just tending to
my plants. I like to think of these plants as my children."

"I was your child once," Maria said.

"You were. I miss those days often. You gave me purpose during those years."

"Please," Maria said, "You did the giving. I was the beneficiary."

"I'd disagree with that," Becks said, "We both gave, and we both received."

"Agreed. Why can't all relationships be like ours?"

"Because without hurtful relationships you can't have special relationships. Comparison gives meaning to everything," Becks said. "Always search for fulfilling relationships, Maria. Preventive medicine."

"For what?"

"For this life."

"Are you getting psychological on me again?"

"Absolutely," Becks replied.

"Good," Maria said, "I needed my daily dose of complexity."

"Will you have a glorious day for me?"

"I promise."

Maria exited the patio and started on the road to Mavrata, turning down her godparents' drive. The day warm now, slowly approaching noon. Mid-morning. All awake, tending to the first tasks of the day. As yesterday, as tomorrow. Inside she found Mrs. Kappatos cooking.

"The boys have left you," Maria said.

"Yes and I'm thankful. The silence is refreshing. I enjoy being alone in my own house."

"You should come to the café for lunch," Maria suggested.

"No, no," Mrs. Kappatos said, "Just some bread for me. I ate too much at name-day yesterday."

Maria helped her godmother cook, wash dishes. They folded clean clothes on the couch together, talking about Maria's garden and cousins from Skala. *She's not Mother, but she helps fill that void, being of the same age, the same generation. Nouna is more open-minded than Mother was. She hasn't even said anything about running around the island with Cole. Mother would have thrown a fit. Silly restraints are the last thing I need right now, and I think my godparents realize it. Amazing they can read me so well after being absent so long.*

They talked on until noon approached, Maria excusing herself, returning to the café as the first early tourists entered the dining room. She brought bread and wine, took orders, chatting about where the guests were from, how long they'd be staying in Kefalonia. Distant strangers entering Maria's life, asking for a meal, please, then returning to their journey. As it had been for her father.

In the dead still of siesta she sat on the veranda with a novel and a glass of wine. She heard the hum of the boat's motor long before they cornered the rocky point at Mavrata. Both bare-chested, Mr. Kappatos driving, Cole in front. When Mr.

Kappatos saw his goddaughter he raised his fist high in the air, similar to a wave but more like a thrusting of triumph — as if the old man had found a lost son at sea, bringing him home forever.

Cole

They motored out from the village shallows as the lights of Zachynthos diminished into the rising sun. The dawn sea. Cole rode in front, the cool salty air upon his arms and across his back. He turned and watched Maria's café along the main street of Katelios, steadily growing smaller as they headed out to sea.

The hum of an outboard motor at dawn, quite meaningless to most folks. Yet for me a remembrance of childhood, sitting in the floor of the johnboat between my father's legs, my father's father in front, pointing at the mallards rising up out of a flooded Mississippi rice field as we sped down a bordering ditch. Woods and waters and fields will always comfort me. Now I can add the sea to my waters.

As they fished that morning, catching synagrida on light tackle rigged with shad-like baitfish, Cole thought: *Will would have loved this. As would my grandfather. But they're both gone now. Accept this new fishing friend and live the day without letting history get in the way. History isn't gonna help you catch more synagrida than Mr. Kappatos. Although you don't know if you could anyway; he's got damn good rhythm to his casts. And you're no saltwater fisherman. Yet you could be if you had a Maria to come home to every night. And Zachynthos to stare at. And that homemade wine to sip on. Greece could become your Mississippi. Or simply your home, bud. It doesn't have to replace Mississippi. There's no mistaking the river levee for Zachynthos. Fish your rod and quit thinking so hard.*

They casted through noon without hint of hunger or thirst. The synagrida never stopped hitting. *Like the crappie inside the levee in spring.* They laughed with little conversation, helping each other when a sizeable hook-up demanded the net. *Sincere fishermen have no need for conversation, even though sometimes it's the finest of all. Like the time above the dam on Greers Ferry, remember that one, when y'all hadn't caught any smallmouth in a while.* The old man told the story of how he met and married your grandmother. *As if some sight or sound had spurned the worn memory inside. You set your rod down, listened with focus, watching the old man's profile.* But he never stopped fishing the entire story. Even during the exciting parts: eloping to Nashville against the wishes of her parents. *Steady casting, as if he spoke of the weather. The old codger had poise, I'll give him that. I never saw him shaken one time. Disappointed but not shaken.*

Sounds a whole lot like another friend of yours. The other one you lost. One young, one old, both preferring worms to spinnerbaits. You can always catch em' on worms, Will used to say. Thing about it is, you were supposed to lose the old man. It was his time by this life's standards, seventy-five years under his belt. But not Willy. He deserved a few more trips to the farm lake in Holly Springs and a chance to call Elsie, tell her that maybe he'd made a mistake. Or the chance to love Mimi this summer.

With two coolers full of synagrida and sore arms they headed back through the afternoon, the sun warm on their shoulders and the smell of fish on their hands. Many a night of his short life Cole had crawled in bed not satisfied with the events of the day, disappointed in himself for watching television or taking a nap when he could have been out among woods or oxbow lakes, or riding horses at Campbell's farm. Yet never when fishing had transpired. If he had fished, the sleep was justified. Even if only an hour before dark, running a top-water bait along a grassy bank at Sardis. So now, with six hours of saltwater fishing between islands in the Ionian, Cole knew the sleep would arrive true as ever. *I just hope it's against Maria's back again.*

The main street of Katelios appeared as they cornered a rocky point, Mavrata sitting on the plateau above. Mr. Kappatos raised his hand to something on shore and Cole looked, searching, finding her there on the veranda, a book across her lap.

Cole rested his face against the skin of her shoulder and told
of his grandfather. Of his scarred, weather-beaten hands. Of the
fishing trips on the Little Red in late fall, how the old man would
stare into his fly-box, speaking the patterns aloud, as if the choice
of what fly to fish with carried the same importance as choosing
a girl, a profession. Maria laughed at this, her frame shaking
within Cole's arms. The smell of her back forced his eyes closed.

He told about hunting mallards in the flooded timber of the
Nixon Creek bottom, Haywood County, Tennessee. How on
clear January mornings the greenheads would light down
through the big oaks, the sunlight illuminating their colors. How
the old man would call them down, chattering at them, hands
cupped around his call until right before they entered range, then
allowing his lanyard to fall, grabbing his gun and raising up while
saying, "Take 'em boys." Shotgun fire echoing through the bottom. The smell of gun smoke on the winter air. His father's
black Lab Luke pounding through the floodwater towards a cripple, fetching it, returning to the blind with head held high, the
bird clutched between his jaws.

How his grandfather would explain why the birds had circled
for so long and for what reason, that something was spooking
them on this side of the blind, that they wanted to light directly

into the wind, that they responded rather well to a feed call when they disappeared over the back of the blind. As if the old man had once been a mallard himself, as if he knew their patterns of thought.

"You're losing me," Maria said in the dark.

"Some things I can't explain. You'd have to be there to understand."

"What's a feed call?"

"Um, do you have a duck call?"

"Not on me," she said, laughing.

"Then you better wait. I'll blow you a feed call one day."

"Promise?" she said.

"Promise."

"Why do you always mention your grandfather, but not your father?"

"You haven't heard?" Cole said.

"What?"

"We're supposed to take our parents for granted."

"Oh yes, I knew that."

"I don't know, Maria. Old men get to me for some reason. The years they've seen. When my father gets up in his sixties I'll probably appreciate him more."

"You're a strange boy, you know that?"

"I've known it for a long time."

"Tell me more, Cole Morgan, and give me your hand."

He offered his hand over the side of her body. She took it, holding it gently, pressing it against her stomach. Cole talked about his mother's paintings, how they always seemed to contain a field of cotton or a rusted barn; honeysuckle along a fence line. No people, Cole said, never. Never has she included a person among her images. Cole paused, rested a moment. He kissed Maria's shoulder before he spoke again.

"I've always wondered why I'm an only child," he said.

"You mean why didn't they have another?"

"Yes."

"That's not of your concern," Maria said, "Nor mine. Although I've wondered it myself."

"What were we?" Cole asked, "Obligations?"

"I don't think that's fair."

"I do," Cole said, "I feel like an obligation met. My folks felt an obligation to have a child, and when the minimum requirements of that obligation were met, they ceased."

"Do you like your current position?" Maria said.

"How so?"

"Holding me, kissing my back."

"Yes."

"Then hush. I won't allow such talk in my bed."

"Yes ma'am," Cole said.

They lay in silence for a good long while; then, in a voice just above a whisper, Maria told Cole the details of her parents' deaths. She spoke respectfully, offering little more than the obvious facts. Father, cancer. Mother, suicide — an incurable sadness. Cole attempted a response but Maria turned and hushed his lips with her finger.

"No more words," she said.

Cole slept, dreamless. When he woke to the first light of Kefalonia Maria lay facing him, strands of black hair caught in the corner of her lips. He smiled and thought of kissing her mouth. Then he slept again.

During siesta they drove in the jeep along the southern shore of the island, the road to Poros, boulders rising out of the sea. The sky clear, mainland Greece present on the distant horizon, the farthest imagination of the eyes. Several times the road narrowed to the jeep's width, Cole asking Maria what happened when travelers met at these points. She shrugged her shoulders and Cole laughed aloud, commenting on the glorious simplicity of island folks.

"We appreciate your approval," Maria said.

They parked along the docks at Poros where fishermen cleaned their boats and messed with tackle and ropes in the afternoon sun. Maria spoke to them in Greek and they laughed, responded. Cole understood nothing but smiled as if not a stranger. As if he could be from this land. Maria took his hand and led him across the street to a bar. Dark and cool, a bartender reading a newspaper, folding it shut as they entered. Maria ordered two beers and the barman nodded. They sat at the bar and sipped the cold beer. Maria spoke to the barman, then the barman said something to Cole. Maria spoke and Cole heard some form of "America."

"Ah," the barman said. He offered his hand and Cole took it. "Hello."

"Hello," Cole said.

"Where from in America?"

Cole pointed with the lip of his bottle to a Jack Daniel's mirror that hung on the wall behind. The barman turned.

"Tennessee?"

"You got it."

The barman shook his head as he walked to the other end of the bar, as if the thought of Tennessee had forever been nothing more than imagination, now made real by a visitor who called the place home. He grabbed his newspaper and opened the screen door that led to a deck, speaking to Maria over his shoulder in Greek.

"Where's he going?" Cole said.

"To read his paper."

"The beer is sweet and cold."

"I know."

"Not many things better than beer in the afternoon."

"It's not bad," Maria said. "That's the first time I've heard you claim Tennessee over Mississippi."

"I saw the mirror."

Maria nodded. "So the fishing yesterday was glorious?"

"The fishing yesterday was glorious."

"Who caught more?"

"Your godfather. But just wait 'til I get him on the farm lake in Holly Springs."

"Right," Maria said, "Nouna can barely get him to Athens.

Another country would take an act of God."

"I used to be like that," Cole said.

"But now you're a traveler."

"A traveler," he said, raising his bottle. Maria tapped it with hers.

"Stin eiya mas," she said.

"Cheers."

Friends. You can hear it in our tones, our ease. Although the thought of being more than friends visits you often. Especially when she lets you kiss her back and lie in the outline of her body. Not so many friendships carry such benefits. Something is keeping her from allowing it to go further, from releasing her heart. Maybe it's because you leave in several days. It proves much easier to get over a friend that you didn't touch than one you did. Those tend to involve tears. Tears were involved with Lily's departure, weren't they old bud? And several nights thereafter. And you imagine, several nights to come. Even with all the regret I do hope she wins. I'd pay money to watch her on stage, to know that the days of her life are spent as she wishes. Our hopes should always run parallel to those we've loved. Even when they've left us. May she win ten thousand Tonys. Then my loneliness will carry significance, and I can be characterized as the old boy who the famous actress left. For a lonely cat you sure are keeping nice company, he thought, watching Maria sip her beer.

They finished and Maria laid the money on the counter. They drove home the back way, through the southern mountains, the villages of Tzanata and Agia Irini and Agios Georgios built into the cliffs as if those who first discovered such views never wanted to see the world another way. In Pastra children played a form of hopscotch on the sidewalk. Two women in aprons sitting on a porch, smoking and talking. Maria hollered yassus to them as the jeep passed.

"What if I told you that Kefalonia was similar to small town Mississippi?" Cole said.

"I'd have no reason not to believe you."

"Then Kefalonia is similar to small town Mississippi."

"Noted," she said, reaching and touching the inside of his forearm as she'd done on the road to Fiskardo.

They dropped down off the mountain, through Markopoulo, turning on the road that ran along the plateau, passing Mavrata and the last descent onto the plain of Katelios, eye-level with the sea again. Maria pulled down the Kappatoses' drive. The couple sat in wrought iron chairs next to the garden, Maria and Cole joining them, telling about their drive to Poros and back. Maria spoke in Greek of who she saw at the docks. Cole sat and listened as the three discussed these people from their land who they knew in the same way they knew the land itself. He understood. *The separation between land and people is paper thin if present at all.* Mr. Kappatos commented in broken English about catching more synagrida than Cole, Cole smiling, Maria responding in Greek, and Mr. Kappatos rolling his head back in laughter. A slight breeze coming down off the mountains beckoned the first hint of dusk, shadows creeping across the stony fields.

"I must get back to the café," Maria said, rising, kissing her godparents, offering her hand to Cole where he sat in the grass. He took it a moment, a bit surprised by the indiscreet display of emotion. Mrs. Kappatos turned her head as if she didn't see, like some voice only heard by her had called from the distance.

"I'll drive you," Cole said.

"No. I've been in that machine enough today. I'll walk."

"All right."

She headed down the gravel drive. All three sat silent, watching her departure. As if committing the image to memory should the girl enter their lives no more.

Without waking her he rose and clothed himself and slipped
on his boots, exiting through the window just as he'd come the
night before. Again there had been no touching save their bodies
in sleep. A kiss on her shoulder before he closed his eyes. She
squeezing his hand as he told stories in the dark.

The western world remained black as he hurried down the
side street through town, crawling through a break he'd made in
the fence for the dawn returns to his guest house. Halfway across
the field that led to his quarters Cole turned through the
mesquite shrubs and started up the rise to the plateau. He
climbed steady and focused, as if certain some prize or revelation
lay in wait. The rock steepened and the boy bent over, crawling
with both hands and feet, gripping the shrubs and pulling himself
along. Several times he stopped, looking back over his shoulder,
the village of Katelios waiting silently for another day, another
sun. He picked out Maria's cottage and pictured her there, still
sleeping amid his scent, hopefully rolling over into the warm
depression he'd created in the night.

Upon the hill sat a church, old and white. Crumbling along
the edges. Weeds grew up the walls, the door torn away. Cole
walked over and gazed inside. Empty save a small wooden cruci-
fix hanging in the center of the far wall, the space no larger than

Maria's bedroom. He tried to imagine when the last service here might have been, if and why it had been abandoned. He ran his fingers through his hair, rubbed the sleep from his eyes, went back out into the dawn. The eastern sky reigned grey, hints of shine reflecting off the rocky summit of Ainos.

The boy sat on the front step of the church with chin held high and eyes wide open. Yet he prayed. Mostly thanks for the obvious blessings of his life.

Cole spoke his thanks for this land, this Kefalonia. *We think of other countries as so distant, so foreign. Yet a few days has me wondering if I could call it home. This island, these people. And then there's Maria.* Cole lowered his forehead upon the crown of his knee, closed his eyes. Whether or not his next thoughts constituted prayer mattered little, for they were kind and humble, and they contained the people of his short life: *Will, Lily, Smitty. Maria.* He remained silent for a good long while then rose and dusted his jeans off and walked to the edge of the hill: the encompassing sea, light of day now pouring over the mountains, a new wind stirring the sage grasses. *I don't have to understand it. I just have to live it.*

He made his way back down the steep rise, then across the field to the guest house. He changed clothes and grabbed his personals, walked over to the house and let himself into the kitchen. Silent and dark, the Kappatoses still sleeping. He walked to the bathroom and bathed, shaved off the several day stubble he'd allowed. When he returned to the kitchen Mrs. Kappatos stood in the grey light from the window peeling a tomato.

"Good morning Cole," she said.

"Mornin' Mrs. Kappatos."

She nodded and motioned him to the table, following with a glass of juice and a half-loaf of bread with a saucer of olive oil. Then she brought a tomato and sliced apricots, humming as she worked some pleasant ballad.

"Eat, eat, eat," she said to Cole.

"Yes ma'am, I shall."

Mr. Kappatos came down the stairs and patted Cole on the back. He fetched a plate and joined him, tearing off a piece of bread and running it through the oil. Mrs. Kappatos brought a pitcher of wine and the old man poured a tumbler half-full and drained it. Then he raised the empty glass to Cole.

"My juice," Mr. Kappatos said.

Maria

She came down the steps of the café and climbed into the jeep, setting the basket on the back seat. She lowered her sunglasses and looked into Cole's face.

"What's for lunch?" he asked.

"Just drive, Cole Morgan. You'll find out soon enough."

"Yes ma'am."

They rode the plateau toward Argostoli, in silence, Maria never removing her hand from Cole's arm. The sea rippled in the summer wind. A distant ferry navigated towards the island, bringing folks from the mainland. Maria waved to pedestrians as they meandered through the roadside villages. She looked to the faces of her people. *I know they're wondering who this boy is. I wouldn't be running around the island with Cole if my parents were alive. I guess tragedy gives us an excuse to act with complete truth, naturally and without care of the judgments of others.*

I haven't thought much of them in the last days. This boy has kept my attention elsewhere. Healing carries an element of releasing. Forgetting. Yet it feels more like betrayal. But you're not betraying them, Maria, you're only living. If the burdens of the past year remained as intense as during the funeral, then there would be no life. No soul can carry such weight. Just look at your mother's decision. Her heart failed to handle loss even through an afternoon.

"Please ma'am," Cole said, "Inform me of your thoughts."

"Guess."

"The Brit. Keane-boy?"

"No."

"Me?"

"No."

Cole looked to the sea in contemplation, driving the mountain road as if he'd done it all the afternoons of his life.

"Your folks?" he said.

"Yes."

"Sadness?"

"I don't know what you call it. It's the first time I've thought of them in days, thanks to you."

"I'll accept the blame."

"I just feel like I should be crying all the time," she said. "Do you understand?"

"If you only knew."

"What's keeping me from knowing?"

Cole looked to Maria's face. "I'll tell you about it," he said, "Let's just ride and look at the sea right now."

"Okay," she said.

They turned inland at Perata, through the villages of Mitakata and Troianata, climbing and dipping through the interior mountains, herds of goats blocking the road at several passes, their neck-bells chiming in the still summer afternoon. Cole hollered at them as would an American cowboy, and Maria laughed. *It would be nice if he stayed the entire summer. Or for good. Don't act like it takes so very long to become fond of a boy. It took one night with Keane. The heart believes as it wishes no matter how many defenses your mind installs. What a glorious defense you installed with Keane. To dismiss the possibility simply because you were from somewhere and he from elsewhere. Real noble of you, Maria. Allow slight difficulty to overcome honest love. A real warrior you are. Of course, the difficulty of it flowed from your parents being alive and wanting you to marry a Kefalonian. You might have stayed with the old Brit if you'd known of the tragedy of the coming year.* Then she thought: *Keane doesn't even know about my folks. I should write him a letter. I wonder if he'd even respond. Oh, you know him, he'd respond. He'd respond beautifully and honestly and it would make you fall in love with him again. As if you ever quit. Is that how it works? Do you continue loving those you've left behind, simply choosing another to spend your days with yet never releasing the feelings of yesterday? Does the heart carry such capacity, such room? Or does it evict when a new tenant moves in?*

You're trying to allow Cole here to move in, aren't you Maria? But his soon departure makes you weary. Loss is getting a bit old. You're ready for a little gain in your life. And not the temporary kind. For so long you put off stability and permanence, but now they're looking

quite attractive. Yet you'd probably try to rid yourself of them the
moment they came into possession. What was that you used to believe:
We only want that which we can lose at a moment's notice. So that's
why Cole here captivates your attention. You know that you're going
to lose him. As he drives you down into the valley of the patron saint,
he is loss, sitting there as you clutch his arm. You've already lost him
and it makes him beautiful, dramatic. What a rough way to live,
Maria. What a damn rough way.

They passed the church and went down the road a little ways,
Maria stopping him at a large tree surrounded by a plot of grass
and flowers. A white cross painted on the massive trunk.

Maria fetched the blanket and basket and walked across the
road. She spread the blanket on the grass and sat, one leg tucked
under her. Cole followed and lay on his back, staring up into the
maze of branches broken by patches of blue sky. Down the road
folks strolled through the courtyard of the church. A couple
passed them on bicycles.

Maria gazed over the fields dotted with olive bushes at the
mountains which separated the interior valley from the sea. At
the church, which stood so striking on the rural landscape, as if a
journeyman without destination or desire could come down from
the mountains and see this church and know that this was the
place he'd been looking for all along. That he could rest now.
Possibly build a little house where a solitary yet hopeful life could

be led, a life where the sun rises daily over the same rocky summit and sets over the same directionless sea. *I will never leave*
again. I feel the land infiltrating me like water on a dry September
afternoon when you haven't drank for hours. I don't think I can leave
a land within which my parents lay. Before, yes, because they walked
and worked and played upon its surface and I always knew they'd be
standing on the terrace at the airport, waving when I'd fly in from
England. But now they're a part of the land in a way they've never
been before. The truest way, I guess. Burial is too fitting. To place a
body within the land upon which it for so long tread. A body, the land.
A body within the land. We keep the land and then the land keeps us.
How kind of it, to take care of us like that. To be our resting place. I
doubt the sea would be so kind. No, the sea would not allow such
peaceful rest. It would continue to torment, carrying us through waves
and currents and in the wake of hungry fish. The sea would be no
place to spend an afterlife. I would prefer the point at Mavrata, next
to the church, alongside those two who gave me my very birth.

"You're getting worse than me," Cole said.

"Quiet places spur the thoughts, don't they?"

"Naturally."

"When I used to take the train down to London, and walk the
busy streets, and look in all the nice stores at clothes even though
I never had the money to buy anything, I never did much thinking.
But on the return trip, staring at the passing countryside, there

was no escape from the thoughts. And in my dorm room, when the only sound came from the chiming of the bells up the road at the Durham cathedral, I thought of every person and experience my past held."

"I understand," Cole said. "At football games in Mississippi in late fall, ten thousand people crowd and picnic under a grove of trees, and drinking beer and walking among them and waving and slapping fives to friends, you don't do any damn thinking at all. But the next day, on Sunday afternoon, when the town settles again and your roommate's off fishing, and there's no girl to call to come watch a movie, all that's left is thought. And sometimes it's not so pleasant."

"And then someone dies."

"Yes. Sometimes. Sometimes someone dies. Then you think even when it's loud and people surround you, and they wonder why you have such a distant look on your face."

"We have it all figured out," Maria said.

"How simple that was," Cole said.

"It's been a strange year so far," she said, "For me anyway."

"And also for me."

"I have to admit, when you come to the café in the afternoons to see me, I smile and wonder who the hell you are as you approach."

"Oh yeah, well, when I wake in the mornings against your back I have to remind myself what country I'm in."

"Surreal I guess you'd call it," Maria said.

"Maybe. Maybe not, though. Maybe we just underestimate this life. Maybe we simply fail to consider how vast the possibilities are because our everydays dull our imagination."

"So you're saying that your time here isn't really that special."

"Not at all," Cole said, "There's no doubt Kefalonia and you are special. It's just that maybe you're not unique. When I go back and tell this story, my friends will shake their heads in disbelief, but why? They'd say because it was such a unique trip. But you are merely a girl in a land that has a name attached to it. Just as I am a boy from a land with a name attached to it. So you have big damn blue sea, and I have a muddy river. But in the end we're nothing more than a boy and a girl playing in the afternoons and falling asleep together in the evenings. There's no reason to get all worked up over that and call it a storybook tale simply because we come from different places and sleep next to the sea."

"Well you don't have to take all the drama away."

"Okay," Cole said, "I'll leave in how pretty you are."

"Thank you."

"Anytime."

Maria fetched a bottle of wine from the basket. She poured two cups and handed one to Cole. He raised it to hers.

"Stin eiya mas," she said.

"Cheers."

"Everyone picnics before the football game?" Maria said.

"One big slap-happy picnic."

"Strange."

"Why?"

"I don't know," Maria said, "I'm just having trouble picturing it in my head."

"Just as I had trouble picturing Kefalonia in my head all the years my parents came and left me behind. But that doesn't mean it didn't exist. And it doesn't mean it's necessarily strange. Just because you haven't seen something before doesn't mean it's strange, it just remains a fiction."

"So you were a fiction before I saw you," she said.

"Yes. A good-looking, well rounded fiction."

"Quite confident this afternoon."

"It's your fault," Cole said, "I figure I must be doing something right if a girl such as yourself would rather spend her siestas with me than a pillow."

Maria picked a blade of grass, twirled it and flicked it off into the slight breeze coming down through the valley. "See, that doesn't count as a compliment. Compliments must be completely sacrificial by the giver. The giver cannot benefit from the compliment."

"Then there would be no compliments at all," Cole said. "People don't really care if you know that you're beautiful or not. They simply want you to like them, so they tell you."

"That's a wonderful attitude."

"Pessimistic but real."

"Well, Cole, you're on an island in the midst of the Ionian, there's no reason to be real."

"Okay then: All compliments flow from the goodness of the human heart."

"That's better," Maria said, "Now let's break some bread."

They ate tomatoes and feta cheese, olives. Cole tore pieces of bread and ran them through a dish of tzaziki. Maria told him about her years in England, how difficult it was to no longer hear the language of her native land.

"Our homes only become unique when we leave them."

"Were you homesick?" he asked, "Did you consider coming home?"

"Not seriously," she said. "I had too much pride. Even if I had wanted to return I wouldn't have let myself." She sipped her wine and looked toward the church. "Anyway, I met Keane after I had been there only a few weeks. So I guess he took care of any homesickness."

"Must have been quite a cat?"

"It wasn't difficult to look at him, if that's what you're saying. I bet that Lily girl has turned some heads in her day."

Cole stared down into his lap. He shook his head. "She turned mine," he said.

"Her hair?" Maria asked.

"Dirty blond."

"Eyes?"

"I don't know. We often argued about them. I thought them more blue; she green."

"Can I ask you something, Cole?"

"Yeah Miss Maria, you can ask me something."

"Do you ever feel like you missed your chance? I mean, do you think by losing this Lily you lost your chance?"

"At what?"

"I don't know. Happiness. Companionship."

The hour bells chimed at the Church of the Patron Saint Gerasimos.

"No Maria, I don't. Lonely has more than one cure out there."

They packed up the picnic basket and placed it in the jeep and walked out through a field of low grape bushes. Cole meandered through the rows, squatting down, raising up between the bushes and making a funny sound. Like a child. Popping up here, then squatting down and moving a few rows over, popping up there. Maria picked up clods of dirt and tried throwing them at Cole when he rose up randomly around the field, but the boy was too fast, leaning down and disappearing before the scattering dirt sprayed the place he'd been. After a while Cole worked his way behind her, coming up out of the shaded depths of the grape bushes to squeeze her waist. Maria let out a shriek.

"Quit making me act like a girl," she said.

"You need to act like a girl every once in awhile. I act like a boy sometimes."

"You act like a boy all the time."

"I take offense to that. If I was a boy then I'd be complaining about you never rolling over to face me in the night."

"Ah," Maria said, "A little truth escapes the boy."

"I was only playing."

"No you weren't," Maria said, "I heard the tone. It's okay. The answer is simple. I wouldn't trust myself if I rolled over to face you."

"Well," Cole replied, "It's a simple answer. But hardly suffi-cient. May I ask an extremely shallow question?"

"Yes."

"What do you have to lose?" Around them the mountains stood still and lifeless in the afternoon. A car could be heard motoring up one of the mountain roads. "I'm sorry," Cole said, "I shouldn't have asked it. You aren't required to explain everything."

"It's all right," Maria said. "It's my heart more than me. I'm just tired of loss. Tired of people leaving. And I know you're going to leave. Loving you would simply make your departure too difficult."

"I didn't say anything about loving me."

"I know what you said. And you know what I said."

Cole nodded. He took her hand and led her down one of the rows, out of the field, across a grove of trees to the jeep. He opened the passenger door for her, as he would do on a Mississippi date. He shut the door gently. She grabbed the front of his shirt.

"Don't regret me," she said.

"Come again."

"I'm scared of disappointing you."

"You're not disappointing me," Cole said. "You could never."

"You think too much of me. I'm not so special. You're just caught up with the island. I wasn't so special in England."

"This Keane thought so," Cole said. Maria stared down into her lap, pinched the material of her skirt.

"That was simply youth."

"I don't buy that," Cole said, now leaning on the windowless jeep door. "I don't buy the youth excuse. All we are is how many years we've lived. Age doesn't bring greater intensity to the pain. The heart has no use for age. The sixteen year old girl who loses her boyfriend and cries in her bedroom feels the same hollow pain as the grey-haired Greek widow who loses her husband to cancer."

Cole stepped back from the jeep. He put his hands in his pockets then ran them through his hair. He squatted on the road, picked up a stone, hurled it skipping down the asphalt. "I'm sorry for that," he said. "I wasn't talking about your mother. It just came out. I wasn't belittling her situation."

"I know you weren't," Maria said. "Your words make sense, Cole. They make a lot of sense. Although I've forgotten what we were talking about in the first place."

"Well it started with me trying to persuade you to face me in the night, but then I got all noble and started with the speeches. You'll have to forgive me."

"Your speeches are lovely, southern boy."

"How do you understand that? How do you know to call me southern boy?"

"You forget how well-read I am. Faulkner, Welty, even the cowboy man, what's his name, McMurtry. I have a picture in my head of the American south. And the boys it contains."

"Do I match?" Cole asked.

"In looks, yes. With your brown boots and blue jeans. I'm not sure otherwise. How shameful it would be for someone to pre-conceive how an entire people are, within."

"Especially since we're all the same, within."

"You'll have to convince me of that one."

"Convince you I shall."

"You almost sounded like Keane, there, for a moment."

"Oh Lord, I'm being compared now." Cole stood, pulled the sleeves of his shirt above his upper arms, flexed his muscles.

"Stop it," Maria said, laughing, "Someone will see you. And I'll never take you seriously again."

"Promise?"

"Let's go. I'm tired of all these words."

They drove slowly up the mountain road out of the valley, Maria turning to watch the church become smaller and smaller. She could make out the black robes of nuns walking in the courtyard. Maria placed her hand on Cole's forearm. *I know he likes that. I can tell through his silence. Boys fall silent when they're at peace. Loud boys usually tend to be unhappy. Keane was outgoing but calm, his words unhurried and sincere. He always got quiet when I'd scratch his neck and shoulders. It hurts to think about him with someone else, this redhead, walking through Covent Garden after work, holding hands, getting a bite of early supper and sipping on a glass of beer.*

London can be a fine place to care for another.

But Kefalonia ranks quite high also, and this boy, this Cole Morgan from Mississippi or Tennessee, wherever he wants to be from, is nothing short of a fine summer surprise. So quit with your weakness about Keane. Be strong, Maria. Keane went from a tan, black-haired island girl to a boring English blue-blood. He couldn't be happy. But you know he is, don't you? Keane would never settle out of loneliness or convenience, no, you know him too well. He cares for this girl if he spends time in public with her. There's something to her; has to be. Her heart probably isn't scared of love for one thing, unlike the incompetent muscle you possess.

"What are you thinking about?" Cole asked.

"My incompetent heart."

"Glad to know I don't possess the only one."

"If you tell me why your heart is incompetent, I'll tell you why mine is."

Cole looked at Maria then back at the road; at the sea as it appeared in the distance.

"My heart is only incompetent part of the time," he said. "Other times it proves quite impressive."

"Is that so?" Maria said.

"Yes. The problem is that it tends to become incompetent when another heart is involved."

"You act as if that's a unique affliction."

"No, I realize it's a wide-spread disease. I've just been suffering for a good long while. The doctors can't seem to find a cure for my particular strain."

"This Lily," Maria said, "This girl who supposedly left you. If she called you tomorrow and said she was coming home, to Mississippi, and that she loved you and no longer wanted to be apart from you, ever, would you welcome her back with open arms?"

"If I say yes will you still allow me to sleep against your back?"

"Yes I will."

"The answer is no."

"You lie to me."

"No," Cole said, "But I will clarify. If she called from Boston and said these things my pride would rear its ugly head and I'd probably give her some tough lines about how I've moved on and how it might be difficult to go back to the way things were. But, if I was home this summer and she showed up on my porch and looked at me and said that she cared for me and wanted to be with me, I would probably take her into my arms. Yes, I would definitely take her into my arms."

"You just confirmed your existence as a boy."

"I suppose this Keane would have said something more sensitive."

"Keane would simply have said no. Whether she called him or showed up on his porch."

"You mean, whether you called him or showed up on his porch."

"Whatever you say."

"Well," Cole said, "I guess this Keane is a bit stronger than me."

Maria reached and fixed the collar of Cole's shirt.

"It has nothing to do with strength," she said, "That's just the way Keane is. When he breaks something he breaks it clean. Completely. No second chances with him. Second chances to him are somehow faulty, impure. He believes that if it doesn't happen on the first attempt then it wasn't meant to be, and moves on."

"I don't agree with that," Cole said.

"I don't either."

"The good parts of me don't even show 'til the second chance."

"I don't know, I've spotted a few since you've been here."

"Yeah?"

"Yeah."

"Talk to me then. Pump me up a little bit. My ego's needed a massage for quite a while now."

They passed through the village of Mitakata.

"Depth," she said.

"Depth?"

"Yes, depth. You possess it. And not simply because of this recent loss."

"Only because I read a lot of books."

"You say that as if it was a curse."

"Sometimes I wonder," Cole said. "Sometimes I wish that I could live more deliberately. Accept my days as they come. Not think about it all so damn much."

"Being able to think about it all is a blessing. Some people rush through this life without even realizing the significance of their stay."

Cole held his hand out to the wind, watching the road pass beneath him and the sunlight spilling over the land in the late afternoon.

"What else?" he asked.

"You kiss my shoulders wonderfully."

"Well, that's the only part of you I get to kiss. Might as well be good at it."

"There's a kindness in you," Maria said. "I don't know if I can describe it only knowing you these two weeks. I know you can be rough, most people can. But there's a kindness in you, a sympathy maybe. Most people only carry their own hurt. I believe you carry the hurt of others as well."

Cole remained silent a good long while. They turned at the village of Peratata, heading southeast towards Mavrata and Katelios, the sea forever on the southern landscape, Zachynthos rising out of the distant waters like some remnant of a country flooded. Maria watched him. His American clothes, the silver rimmed sunglasses, the coal black hair much like her own. *We'd have lovely children. I could probably get most people on the island to believe that he's Greek-American. "Just doesn't speak the language,"*

I'd tell them. But Greek to the core. I wonder if he'd try and take me back to Mississippi, to these cotton fields and bottomlands he keeps talking about. These river levees.

"We act as if we can predict what life will bring us," she said. A goat-herder waved from a sagebrush field.

"Explain."

"Do you think three weeks ago, when I was mourning the death of my parents, I predicted that I'd become friends with an American boy after meeting him in Katelios?"

"I see."

"Same goes for you, Cole Morgan. You didn't even know where you were going. Your folks just put you on the plane and shipped you off."

"That's how it happens."

"How what happens?"

"Our lives," Cole said. "It just sends us places. Or sends people to us. That's what you told me the other day. And it doesn't have to provide a reason for the sending."

"I'll miss you when you leave," Maria said.

"Let's not talk about it."

"It's just as much a part of it all as the sending."

"What?" Cole said.

"The leaving," she said.

"Yes, but you don't have to talk about it."

"Is that your way of saying that you will also miss me?"

"I will also miss you," Cole said.

"Will you miss driving with me on the road to Katelios, or will you miss kissing my back, or will you miss eating bread and tzaziki, or will you miss talking to me at the cafés along the docks at Fiskardo?"

"Can I say all of them?"

"Yes."

"All of them," Cole said, "I will miss all our time."

"Will you miss Nouna's broken English?"

"Yes."

"Will you miss the way Nouno recognizes our affection for each other but says nothing?"

"Yes. But he did say something to me."

"When?" Maria said.

"Before the name-day party. He told me to keep my distance. He didn't think the locals needed to know of our little affair."

"Wise man, my godfather."

"Yes he is. And a hell of a fisherman at that."

Maria looked toward the sea.

"It is big and it is blue," she said.

"It is big, it is blue."

"My father always spoke of the sea as a woman. 'She was mighty fine today,' he would say."

"It has its womanly traits."

"Such as?"

"Well, let's see," Cole said. "Sometimes it's too rough to navigate."

"Good."

"It lures men to distant lands."

"Not bad."

"It's at its prettiest in the moonlight."

"You are quite clever, southern boy."

"Glad to be of service."

They approached Mavrata.

"The birthplace of my parents," Maria said, "And where they returned. Turn here, Cole."

Cole turned down the main street of Mavrata, folks rising from their siesta naps, watering flowers on their patios, a group of men sitting in front of the Kafenio. Maria waved. "They'll be talking about this," she said.

"About what?"

"Maria riding alone with that strange American boy."

"Let them talk."

"Yes, let them talk. You'll be gone soon and they'll forget you."

"Well you don't have to be so rough about it," Cole said.

"I'm rough when I'm sad," she said. The road wound past the church and they started out the other end of town. Dogs played amidst the rubble of an old cottage. Gardens lay along both sides of the road, olive trees and grape vines, tomatoes and cucumbers. Maria pointed to a narrow gravel road.

"There," she said, and Cole turned, the grasses and weeds brushing the sides of the jeep as they eased down the road. Over a rise sat a small white church that faced the sea, as if its cross might be a guide to wayward seamen, as if some Kefalonian sailor who'd been lost amidst the endless sea could mark this church upon this cliff and know that the island was Kefalonia, know that the island was his home. Cole didn't see the graves until they walked around the side of the building. He paused a moment, then went over and sat on the stone wall surrounding the tomb-stones. He stared at the sea and Zachynthos in the distance, small whitecaps rising and disappearing as the wind came down off the island.

Maria watched him, then crawled over the wall and stood before her parents' markers. After a minute Cole turned and watched her. Maria looked up. "This is where they rest," she said. Cole nodded. He rose and walked over, took her hand. She accepted it without hesitation. Cole noted the names, the dates, the Greek inscription written on the grey stone. He didn't ask what it meant.

"It is a beautiful spot, this place."

"I know," Maria said. "Often times I wish it wasn't."

"I understand."

Cole offered his hand yet Becks embraced him.

"You have taken my late afternoon friend away from me," Becks said. "Now I just sit here reading my gardening book, alone, nobody to talk with."

"My sincerest apologies," Cole said.

"You're probably enjoying a break from my rantings," Maria said.

"Oh no, Maria, the turmoil of the young heart is refreshing to us old folks. Now come, you two, I've drawn us a pitcher of wine."

They sat around the wrought iron table, Becks pouring the glasses, Cole nodding in thanks.

"I've met your parents, Mr. Morgan. At the café. Anatole and I walked down for a late supper one night last summer and your folks were eating with the Kappatoses. Your mother is quite beautiful if I may say."

"Thank you," Cole said, "And she thanks you."

"Do they come to Kefalonia every summer?"

"About every other."

"If I remember correctly, Mrs. Kappatos told me that she painted."

"Yes ma'am."

"Famous?"

"No," Cole said. "But she does have a local following around Memphis."

"What does she paint?"

Cole sipped from his wine and looked to Maria as if she might provide an answer.

"Southern country," he said.

"Southern country?"

"Yes ma'am."

"And what might southern country look like?"

"Well, southern country usually has fields of row crop or big woods or muddy rivers. Honeysuckle along fence lines. Cypress brakes."

Becks laughed and looked to Maria, "Can you picture it?"

"Oh, I picture it. I just doubt the accuracy of my imagination," Maria said.

"You'd have to see these places. I couldn't explain them to you. Just as Kefalonia couldn't be explained on a Mississippi patio."

Becks grinned at Maria. "A wise boy you've found."

Cole shook his head. "Your student there is the wise one."

Becks looked at Maria again with fixed eyes, as if making a decision she'd been pondering for a good long while. "Yes, she is. You are wise for recognizing it. Some of the greatest wisdom this world has ever known was simply the recognition of its existence in others." Becks sipped her wine and stared at her lap a moment. "You may take that as a compliment," she said.

"Thank you ma'am. I appreciate that."

"The gate you all came through. There." Becks pointed.

"Yes ma'am?" Cole said.

"That's where your friend Maria stood as a little girl, about seventeen or eighteen years ago, staring at me as I picked plums. No telling how long she'd been standing there before I recognized her. She was as lovely then as she is now."

"I can imagine," Cole said.

"You all stop it," said Maria.

They drank the wine. A slight wind swept across the patio. Cole looked above at the distant sky. Maria watched him, imagining his thoughts. *Still a stranger to me, yet my friend. The boy who kisses my shoulders in the night. Keane would be a bit jealous probably. This American boy, with me, in Kefalonia. He said that he'd give up London to follow me home to this island and I refused him. On practical grounds. Now you're showing this Mississippi boy off all over the island, caution thrown to the wind. Yet it's not the same. I simply found Cole here. I didn't have any say in the matter. Don't try and justify your cowardness in regards to Keane. History is as it stands, Maria.*

"Did you miss her?" Cole asked, "When she left for England?"

"Of course," Becks said, "Terribly. I missed teaching also. Although those last years she taught me more than I taught her."

"Nonsense," Maria said.

"It's true. I once knew about youth. Yet I had forgotten it all. Only a young voice could have reminded me."

"Two weeks is too short a stay," Becks added.

"Agreed," said Cole.

"I came to meet Anatole's parents and never left. Of course at first they weren't so excited about my fair skin and my Greekless heritage." Becks stared ahead, looking at neither Maria nor Cole. As if telling her story to the wind. "You know I've only been back to England a few times in twenty-five years. As if I abandoned the life given me and chose a new one. Wise choice I can say now, years of hindsight on my side. And this island, this sea. Good things to have on your side I tell you. I wish you could have met Anatole. He's in Argostoli for the day."

"Yes ma'am."

"You're here for several more days, correct?"

"Yes ma'am."

"Come by one evening while Maria's working. You can eat supper with Anatole and I."

"I appreciate that," Cole said.

"Be nice to my student, hear?"

"Yes ma'am."

They stood before one another, in the alleyway behind the café.

"Will you kiss me on the mouth once before I leave?"

"No," Maria said.

"Why not?"

"Reason to return," she said. "You know Cole Morgan, I could get used to days like today."

"I could too."

"Will you come and sleep against my back tonight?"

"Of course. Never met a back I wouldn't sleep against."

"Sleeping alone can be quite a lonely thing, can't it?"

"Yes," Cole said, "And we don't even know that we're alone while we sleep."

"I do," she said.

Cole

Summer days that passed as true as the morning wind coming down off the mountain Ainos. And faster even than those of
his childhood, when entire summers seemed to come and go over
the course of an afternoon. Swimming during siesta off the rocks
at Katelios while the rest of the island slept the heat away. Diving
together in unison. Playing the games of children. Then lying on
the warm stone, eyes closed, feeling the white sun bear down
upon them, drifting into sleep then awake again at the touch of
one hand to the other.

When she worked the café he'd go and toil the gardens with
Mr. Kappatos, listening to the sincere broken English about
tomatoes in this kind of heat, about spraying the grapes, about
Cole's father; that he'd made Mr. Kappatos a good bit of money
over the years. "I wish he come more," Mr. Kappatos said one
morning, in a tone of almost sadness, as if realizing that he was in
the late evening of his life. "You and father. Same. Very much
same." It was a statement heard before, spoken through the years
by his father's friends in Memphis, family, even his prep school
buddies. That they possessed similarities in their manner, their
talk, the patience with which they listened. Cole never thought
much of it. It didn't surprise him, though. *If they find us alike, well,*
we come from the same blood. I'm not going to fight it.

Cole knew his father also recognized the similarities. In a way it had driven them slightly apart, fearful of recognizing their own faults in each other. In a way closer, able to understand each other without explanation. They read each other. His old man could tell Cole's sadness by the way he ate his eggs. Happiness by what time he rose in the morning for school. *My old man's got my number. Somebody has to, I guess. Lily had it for a little while. And now possibly Maria. Maybe your number is not so difficult to obtain.*

As the days passed in Kefalonia, he thought less and less of Will. Of Lily. Involuntarily, as if the wind coming off the mountain swept the remembrances away, leaving nothing but life in the village of Katelios: Gardening with Mr. Kappatos; eating breakfast with Mrs. Kappatos; swimming in the late afternoons with Maria; crawling up against her back when the evening neared midnight. He and the old man fished again, catching more synagrida this time, filleting the fish themselves, grilling them on tin foil with lemons and olive oil and eating outside next to the garden with Maria and Mrs. Kappatos. A crimson sun disappearing over the western crest of the island. The wine mild and true.

One morning, driving the jeep alone from the garden in Mavrata back to Katelios, Cole believed that this was his life.

He ate one night with Becks and Anatole, as invited, and they disposed of two carafes of wine while discussing American authors, Cole trying to explain the landscape which had given birth to Faulkner's ghosts.

"We must go," Becks said to Anatole.

"It's no Kefalonia," Cole said. "Muddy fields and big timber and bottomland creeks. No breathtaking sights. But it has soul. I know that sounds a bit dramatic, but it does. It's got plenty of soul."

Becks told the story of her and Anatole, a tale beginning at a small music school in Germany. Cole listened to the contentment in her voice, as if never a doubt had risen over the boy she'd chosen to spend her life with, especially when she witnessed this island from which he came.

"I understand" is all Cole said when she ended. *Maybe I will sound like that one day, when I tell some youth the story of my girl. And my girl tells the story of me. Could Maria be the character in that story? By the way she touches your arm you'd have to say yes, wouldn't you old bud? But would Maria live in Mississippi? Would she fish that oxbow lake inside the levee at Walls and would she canoe the Yocona River and would she sit on a dove stool in the hot September afternoon drinking a cold beer and watching the Tennessee hills cast shadows over sunflowers as birds dipped and soared over the treeline? Or would that be too much to ask?*

And do you really want a replica of yourself, or a girl completely different? A girl like Lily? Old Will could help you with this one. On an evening drive back from the farm lake in Holly Springs, a warm wind swirling in the truck, cold beers between legs, Will laying out all the pros and cons before finally concluding with, "You know Cole, only one thing really matters: Can you wake up in the morning and stand being away from her? If you can stand it, well then, move on. If you can't stand it, well then, go get her. It's not so damn complicated. We just make it that way 'cause we fear regret." When Will had a Mississippi highway and a cold beer and some wind swirling in the truck, the old boy could spout some prophesy. Especially with a day of fishing in his pocket. Those drives will be different now.

But something makes you believe that he'll still be there, with you and Smitty, somewhere in the still blackness of the truck on winter dawns, driving the potholed highways of the Mississippi Delta with a line of grey forming in the east, Smitty spilling coffee on himself and talking about decoy spreads and what kind of wind would blow and the new duck call he'd bought in Memphis at the outdoors show. Something makes you believe that he'll hear your conversations, know your thoughts.

So you've forgotten him here in Kefalonia. It's okay, bud, there's no need to feel guilty. Will has no history here. This is your deal and your deal only. You'll be back to those cotton fields and hardwood bottoms soon. And the old boy will wait. Promise. Especially those last miles of road before Moon Lake.

Not a cloud. No breath of wind. He watched her float through the shallows on her back, the light shining on her skin, eyes closed. He would give anything to know her thoughts. Or possibly not. *Others may not be exactly as you create them, old boy.*

She lifted herself out of the sea and climbed up the rocks, the water dripping from her body, making the stone slippery, climbing with hands and feet like a child. She smiled at him where he lay squinting in the sun. He returned it. She stretched out on the smooth rock and sighed. Down the shoreline tourist children played soccer on the beach. A distant boat made its way toward Zachynthos.

"Do you swim this often back home?"

"No."

"Shame."

"Yep," Cole said. He appeared to bow his head. "You know Maria, I don't even remember the last thing I said to him."

Maria sat up, shielded her eyes from the afternoon sun. Cole had his arms wrapped around his knees, head down, staring between his legs where the water dripped slowly from his bathing suit upon stone.

"Go on," she said.

"I could spend more time with that boy than anyone else. We never tired of each other. We'd camp out at Sardis sometimes for three days straight and never share a cross word. Not even want to leave. Fishing for crappie in the old creek beds. I don't know. I doubt life will ever bring me someone like that again." Cole looked up. "I'm getting over it, though. I feel myself forgetting."

"It's natural," she said.

"I know, but it makes me feel guilty. To recover from a friend like that. I'm afraid that Will can see me now, see the fun I'm having here in Kefalonia, and that he's saying to himself, 'It didn't take Cole long to get over it.'"

"That's just you torturing yourself. You create those thoughts. For a while I only dreamed of my father for some reason, and I started to believe that my mother was mad at me for not dreaming of her."

"My dreams seem to prefer Lily over Will."

"Cole?"

"Yes."

"Can I change the subject a minute? Ask you something about Lily?" Cole nodded, skipped a pebble across the stone and into the water. "Do you long for her to come back?"

Cole skipped another rock.

"I have been but I'm going to stop. There's no point in it. There's no point in longing or wishing over things we can't control. All we can do is live the day. If Lily wants to be a part of those days, well, she's welcome. But I'm not going to keep an eye out for her."

Maria watched him, intently, as if he might clarify or change his response. After several moments of silence she appeared satisfied, or at least appeased, and added: "I'm glad to know you, Cole Morgan."

"Appreciate it."

"Now tell me about Will."

Cole smiled. "Skinny, about my height, dirty blond hair."

"About him, not his features."

"Well, let's see. He caught more lunker bass than anyone I'd ever known. He didn't shoot so great in the rice fields but in the flooded timber he was a dead-eye. Absolutely no fear in regards to girls. None at all. Give him a Maker's and water and he could flirt with the best of them. Loved being single but when he fell he fell hard and fast. I could go on for days. Words are no use, though."

"What was he going to do with his life?"

"Go back to the Delta and farm, probably, with his old man."

"Cole?"

"Yes."

"You didn't tell me how you lost him."

Cole lay back on the stone, stared at the sky. "Wreck. Leaving Moon Lake. We'd been drinking on the lake all day and Willy let the truck get over in the gravel and it was over."

"Just you in the truck?"

"And Smitty. We barely had a scratch on us. Don't ask me

how. Will was gone by the time we found him lying on the road. Right at sunset, too. One of the prettiest I've ever seen. That red Mississippi sky over the levee." Cole stood, walked over to the edge of the rock. He looked into the water with purpose. "We shouldn't have let him drive. Will never could handle it. And we knew that. We knew it. We knew it and we still let him drive."

"Cole?"

"Huh?"

"You just said you were going to quit mulling over things you can't control."

"This is different."

"Why?"

"Because it was in my control. Letting Will drive was in my control. Lily was never in my control."

"Maybe so. But no longer. You can do nothing now. You're helpless and when you realize that you're helpless then you can start to get better, start to forget."

"I don't want to forget."

"I don't mean forget Will," Maria said, "I mean forget how to be sad about it. Just remember him as he was, for the time you had him."

"Maria?"

"Yes."

"The night I lost him. We were all sitting at Fletcher's cabin. Will's parents had come and gone, the emergency vehicles had taken him away. It was just us kids sitting there in the dark of Fletcher's cabin. A few of the girls would stand up and walk outside and cry. You know what happened to me?"

"What?"

"I got hungry. Like I've never been in my life. I went into the kitchen and made myself two of the biggest turkey sandwiches you've ever seen, and I sat down with a tall glass of ice water and ate like it was my final meal." Cole turned and looked at Maria where she sat on the rock. Behind him the sea stretched blue and shining to Zachynthos. "I didn't want to get hungry. Hell, I wanted to stop living for a few days. But I became hungry and then sleepy and when I woke the next morning I was thirsty. And only days after the funeral I had the desire to fish again. Smitty and I went to the farm lake in Holly Springs. A good day, too, I think we caught about twelve lunkers. Three days after my best friend left me I was catching largemouths."

"It happens," Maria said.

"What?"

"Life. The succession of days. At least you possessed some sort of desire. I had to create a dependency in the garden. I forced myself to believe that the garden needed me."

"I didn't have to force myself," Cole said, "I truly wanted to fish."

"That's good."

"No it's not. It's disrespectful and shameful."

"Cole," Maria said, standing, "There's no appropriate ceremony to conduct when someone leaves us. They simply leave. And there's no respectful way to live in the wake of losing someone. Gardening, fishing, working. None of it matters. Do you hear me, Cole? There's no ceremony, and there never will be."

Maria skipped forward and jumped, her body floating in the wind, raising her arms above her head and entering the sea soundless. Cole watched as she swam through the clear shallows, coming up for momentary breaths then going underwater again. After a while she climbed upon one of the low rocks, shaking the water from her hair. Cole hadn't moved. Maria didn't look back at him. She stared off at some unknown point on the sea, as if awaiting a return.

Cole opened the curtains. The grey light of evening. Silence save the wind rustling the sage grasses. A car faintly humming on some high mountain road. He pictured Maria as she worked the café, offering kind words to her guests.

He turned the lamp on and retrieved the story from his bag. *You've got a full hour before Mrs. Kappatos serves supper. You can do this.* He sat down at the desk and read the first words. He knew what they meant. Words that belonged to his life: retrievers, flooded timber, winter dawns, greenheads. *I don't know why these are the things I know about. We are given no choice in the life we're dealt. Maria was dealt the sea, gardens, Katelios. Lily, the theatre. Smitty, Will and I: woods and muddy water. But Will was dealt something else, too, something better than Smitty and I. Although there's not a word I could offer in explanation.*

You know what this boy's going through, don't you Cole? You've been lost in a flooded bottom with a north wind coming down through the big oaks. You know what those naked branches sound like under a grey winter sky. You know how cold it can be with a small leak in your waders, your feet numb, the chill moving slowly up your body until you begin to quiver in an attempt at warmth. All you want is to feel the dry heat off the wood stove back at the camphouse, a cup of coffee, the old retriever nuzzling your leg for an ear scratch. You watch the mallards fly over, so free from such mortal afflictions as cold and direction. You envy them. But you don't think idealistically for too damn long, because your wader legs are filling up with water and the sky's moving toward pitch blackness and there's no ridge in sight. A ridge with some dry old dead branches that you could build a fire with, curl up and sleep in the winter night next to a roaring fire.

Finish this damn story, Cole. This boy deserves a respectful ending as much as anybody else. No matter how it turns out. Your life goes on, so must his. Or end. It doesn't matter. Just finish it.

He took the pen and pressed it to the blank white under the last sentence written. He wrote a page of words, stopped, set the pen down. He leaned back and rubbed his eyes, then stared out the window at this island. This Kefalonia. Then he retrieved the pen and began again.

The wind rose. Curtains fluttered against the wall.

Maria

She leaned against the jeep, watching patiently as Mrs. Kappatos held Cole by the arms. She listened to the words spoken by her godmother, these affectionate phrases used by all when departure is imminent. *They are pleasant, but they always leave us wanting. It would be better to simply embrace and wave. But we never allow such simplicity. We have to muddle it up with attempts at the impossible, such as attaining contentment in goodbyes. We refuse to accept that happiness is not the appropriate emotion for all occasions.*

Maria drew lines in the dusty drive with her feet. Mr. Kappatos spoke of Cole's parents, that they all should return together. Return soon. Cole nodded to the old man, thanked him for the fishing and the mornings in the garden and all the good food and wine. Mr. Kappatos waved his hand across the air, dismissing the thanks as unnecessary. They embraced and Cole retrieved his bag, walking over and tossing it into the back of the jeep.

"Maria, you don't have to bring jeep back today," Mr. Kappatos said, "Use it a few days if you want."

"Thanks Nouno."

"Goodbye Cole," the old man said, his wife standing next.

"'Til next time," Cole said. Mr. Kappatos nodded in affirmation.

High on the road to Mavrata, just before they crested out of sight, Cole turned in his seat and looked back at the valley of

Katelios. It lay as before, and as it would after. The shops and
newsstands along the beach, Maria's café. The window where he
crawled every night. In the distance the rocks where they swam.
The figures of Mr. and Mrs. Kappatos, still standing in the side
yard by the garden, Mr. Kappatos scanning the landscape with
hands upon hips as if deciding how to spend this day of his life.

"Well," Maria said.

"They took me into their home."

"Yes."

"They fed me and gave me wine."

"Yes."

"They are now my friends."

"Yes."

"And that's all. There's nothing else. Further words unnecessary."

"Good boy," Maria said, "Will you do so well after you say
goodbye to me?"

"Probably not. I've been known to get attached to backs I've kissed."

"You'll be fine."

"And you?" Cole asked.

"I'll be devastated," she said. Cole grinned and stared out at
the passing sea.

They passed through the villages on the road to Argostoli.
Maria knew them by heart, around which curves they would
appear, what old men would be sitting on the roadside benches.

She said their names in her mind: *Simotata, Vlachata,*
Moussata, Poriarata.

"This is sad," Cole said.

"What?"

"I recognize things along this road now. I remember them
from our trips to Fiskardo and the valley of the patron saint."

"Why is that sad?"

"Why is that sad?" Cole repeated.

"Yes."

"Because I'm leaving when I'm just starting to learn."

"You should have scheduled a longer trip."

"I didn't know I was gonna be this happy here."

"You should have listened to your mama."

"More so than I'd like to admit," he said.

"Maria?"

"Yes."

"When we talked about Will the other day, on the rocks."

"Yes."

"I hadn't thought of him in several days. Nor have I since."

"Is that a compliment?" she asked.

"I don't know. Maybe."

"To me or Kefalonia?"

"Will you share the honor?"

"Yes," she answered.

"Then to you both. I owe all healing to Kefalonia and Maria Girgiou."

Maria looked over at Cole and touched his forearm. "It's okay not to think about him," she said. "You don't owe him anything, except to live as before."

"Are you going to practice what you preach?"

"Yes," she said.

"Then I will too."

Maria stopped the jeep as a goat tender moved his herd across the road into another field. Random goats belled, chiming as they hurried down through the sage grasses.

"Maria?"

"Yes."

"Can I write you?"

"You can write me."

"Maria?"

"Yes."

"Will you tell Becks and Anatole I'm sorry for not saying goodbye?"

"I will. They enjoyed having you for supper the other night."

"How do you know?"

"They told me."

"Maria?"

"Cole."

"Will you think of me when you swim by the rocks?"

"I promise."

"That's all I can ask."

"Yes, that's all you can ask," she said.

They turned off the main road at Peratata, coming down through the last hills to the airport, swiftly passing through the villages of Travliata, Metaxata, Kaligata, Domata, Svoronata. This Maria Girgiou, this Cole Morgan. Riding in silence. Maria saw the airport approaching, the sea forever behind. She swallowed difficultly and tucked her hair behind her ears.

"I feel like I just got here," Cole said.

"I know."

"I feel like there's something we should say, something we should do."

"There's nothing to say, Cole."

She pulled in under the airport portico. They got out of the jeep, Cole retrieving his bag and setting it on the curb. "Don't come in, okay?" he said.

"Okay. If you don't want me to," she said. "Wait." From under the driver's seat she pulled something wrapped in tin foil and a small water bottle filled with wine. "Yanni's bread and Nouno's wine. For the ride."

"Bread and wine, huh. Kind of religious. I thank you."

"Accepted," she said.

"No ceremony to a departure."

"Right."

"You said it."

"I know," she said, "It's true."

"Okay then. No ceremony Maria Girgiou."

"No ceremony Cole Morgan."

They embraced. A pain in Maria's chest. There was no kiss. She held the back of his neck for several moments. She watched him pick up his bag and walk through the doors of the airport. Through the glass he faded into a crowd of people.

At Metaxata she pulled off the road next to a small house and climbed into the backseat. She lay with her head against the armrest. Half an hour she lay there, staring at the encompassing sky. Then the small plane coming into sight, rising toward Zachynthos.

She heard a door slam and leaned forward. An old woman with a basket of wet laundry came out of the house. She began hanging the clothes on the line before noticing Maria. They spoke in Greek.

"Yassu," the old woman said.

"Yassus."

"What are you doing?"

"Watching a plane leave."

"Did you know someone on the plane?"

"Yes," Maria said.

"Planes," the woman said, shaking her head, "I was thirty-seven before I ever left the island."

Maria watched as the old woman hung the clothes. A simple task, yet necessary. "Do you mind if I sing?" the old woman asked.

"Do you mind if I listen?" Maria said. The woman began. Maria leaned back and closed her eyes. The ballad told of Kefalonian villagers held captive in the bowels of foreign ships. Realizing they would never return, the captives sang of the island's beauty.

Of how they would miss their only home.

Cole

*N*othing more honest than a highway. They take us to the same
places. Pass the same cotton fields, the same bayous, the same share-
cropper cabins. Never misleading. You know they are up to the journey,
always. Highways have no care of time or season. No care of people.
Only true, only focused. Unaffected by any triviality. Even by the
death of a young Mississippi boy who I cared for, who I miss. You'll be
there soon, buddy, don't try and prepare for it. It'll come when it comes.

Jonestown, Mississippi. He watched the blacks in the store
parking lot drinking malt liquor out of brown paper sacks; a lone
cop resting in his cruiser. Children chasing each other in oak
shaded yards, jumping the railroad tracks with their hand-me-down
bicycles. Two white farmers leaning against the bed of an
old pickup, chatting.

Fields again, green cotton darting away toward distant
timberlines. The hot summer air swirling in the truck, back
sweating, arm hanging out the window. Sometimes raising his
hand to the wind, for no reason save that he had always done it
since he was a boy and if he lived to be an old man well he'd do it
then too. Across US 61, down the back road leading to Moon
Lake, turning right at the beer store, Smitty pulling the truck
over on the gravel shoulder.

They got out. Smitty hopped up on the hood and lit a smoke.

Cole leaned against the door. Where they had lain before stood rows of cotton, green and full. A good-looking crop. In the gravel before the truck lay nothing. No mark or indication that a boy met his last afternoon there. A boy who'd been kissing a pretty Clarksdale girl all day. A boy who could catch bass even with an east wind. The boy who had brought Lily across his path, and, in a way, Maria. *You'd of never gone if it hadn't a' happened.*

Cole nodded to himself. He reached down and picked up a rock and hurled it out over the field. "Let's go catch some lunkers, Smit'," he said.

An old woman at the beer store made them ham sandwiches. She wrapped them in oil paper and when she handed them to Cole she wished them luck on the lake. "Spinners been workin' good around the cypress knees," she said. "My husband caught a stringer of slabs yesterday. Green spinners with small spoons."

"Appreciate that," Cole said. Back in the truck he told Smitty what the woman had said.

"Spinners in this heat?" Smitty said.

"That's what she said."

"I don't believe it."

"I'll make you believe," Cole said.

"We'll see about that."

They launched Smitty's johnboat and cranked the old fifteen horse motor and eased across the lake. A white hazy sky stood watch over the Mississippi afternoon. Ski boats filled with college folks hummed at the far end of the lake. Laughter could be heard across the water when the wind died.

"We probably know everybody down there," Smitty said.

"I don't feel like it today," Cole said.

"I don't either."

At the point of Mohead Island, Smitty killed the motor. Cole used the skulling paddle to move them closer to the cypress knees. They both rigged green spinners and went to casting, the slightest breeze out of the west keeping the mosquitoes at bay. Cole landed three small ones in the first ten minutes. Not a word between the boys until Smitty reeled in a four pounder.

"Quality not quantity, that's always been my motto," Smitty said. Cole shook his head.

They settled into fishing with few sounds: the reel spinning, the lure hitting the water, moans from cattle grazing on Mohead Island. The simple peace of fishing with a friend on water that holds history. Memory. Girls, laughter, sunsets over the river levee. Cole had never shown Smitty the words he'd written about Moon Lake, yet no matter. Smitty knew their meaning without ever reading a word.

After a while Cole set his rod down, retrieved his sandwich and a beer from the cooler. He sat in the bottom of the boat, using a lifejacket for a backrest. He watched a pickup move along the lake road, disappearing behind cabins and stands of trees then reappearing upon its route. He watched Smitty cast. He took the last bite of his sandwich and crumpled the oil paper and drank from his beer and told Smitty. He told Smitty everything. When he finished he grabbed the paddle and skulled them farther down the bank.

"She never kissed you?"

"Nope."

"What for?"

"Don't know, bud, but I suspect she had a good reason."

"And she was fine?"

"As frog hair."

Smitty shook his head. "In the middle of the sea, huh? And you could see other islands?"

"You could see other islands," Cole said.

"Your folks know how to do it, don't they?"

"I guess so."

"Well, there won't be any forgetting that one."

Cole casted and reeled in slowly. "No, there won't."

"And you just left?" Smitty said.

"Just left. What else was I gonna do?"

"Opposite of leave, bud. Stay."

"Yeah. Like I just make those kind a' decisions daily."

After a moment Smitty nodded. "Guess you're right. Just

doesn't seem right for something like that to happen and not be able to do anything about it."

"I hear you, bud, I hear you."

They fished the entire south shore of Mohead Island, picking up a few here and there. Smitty cranked the motor and they headed back across the lake, working the docks south of Jenny McIntire's cabin. Cole rigged his cane pole and started jigging for crappie. He caught four slabs off one dock.

"You got the idea, bud," Smitty said, then, "It's good to have you in my boat again."

"Don't get sentimental on me, hear."

"You were gone too long."

"Hell, two weeks."

"Well who else am I supposed to fish with?" Smitty said.

"You telling me that I've got to hang around the rest of my life just so you have somebody to fish with?" Cole said.

"You got it."

The afternoon moved toward dusk. The wind lying, the mosquitoes hovering in the shade. The cypresses casting their shadows out across the murky water. The haze fading, leaving a patient blue sky. The land all crisp and golden in the Mississippi shine. The hum of a crop-duster flying the fields around Fryars Point.

"Cole?"

"Smitty."

"Today. Up on the road. What went through your mind?"

"How good the crop looks," Cole said.

"Seriously?"

"Not much of anything, I guess. Driving over I was scared. Thought it'd be pretty tough. But there wasn't much to it."

"I thought surely one of us would get upset or something. It didn't even get to me."

"We're getting over it, Smitty. It's just a road where something happened. It'll be there as long as we come over here and it'll mean less and less."

"You think we ought to put up a cross or a marker or something?"

"Shut the hell up," Cole said.

"Why? What's wrong with that?"

"Will would hate that. He'd hate us makin' a big deal over it. It's over, Smitty, it happened and now it's over."

"It doesn't seem right for it to be over," Smitty said.

Cole hooked his jig to one of the eyes of the cane pole. He set the pole in the bottom of the boat and looked out over the lake, the sun barely touching the river levee now, the laughter of youth still echoing from the sandbar.

"No ceremony, Smitty."

"What?"

"No ceremony."

"What the hell does that mean?"

"It means that putting up a marker won't help," Cole said. "It means that there's nothing we need to do. You just have to let people leave, Smitty. You just have to let them leave."

Smitty shook his head. He looked down at the rod in his hand. He clicked the reel and casted, the lure splashing next to an old pier stake. Cole watched him methodically retrieve the lure, feeling its weight, moving it through the water as he imagined a fish would want to see it. Smitty casted again, the same rhythm, retrieving with more concentration now, more desire. Then again.

"You just keep fishing, Smitty Cook," Cole said.

Evening found them on Highway 6: shirts off, windows down, the mild summer air swirling in the truck as they topped the low hills coming into Oxford. Smitty asked questions about Kefalonia, Cole offered the answers. The day at its end, grey night spreading over cotton fields and pine woods. A star evident in the eastern sky.

Past the county line, the distant lights of Oxford glowed over the treeline. This place where they'd come together. Three boys. Lily. *In a place, together.* In the roadside gravel an old black man walked, a garden hoe propped over his shoulder. From some day of manual labor. No thumb outstretched to passing cars, no hurry in his step. As if he had a long way to go before deciding on a destination.

She folded the papers and placed them back in the envelope. The letter, the story. She closed her eyes and leaned back in the chair and swallowed. The envelope lay in her lap, held by both hands.

After a while she rose and went to the window. Gardens lined the fence, manicured grass beneath old midtown oaks. Sunlight filtered down through the trees, sprinkling the lawn with dots of shine. She went outside, sitting in a rod iron chair under the oaks and reading the letter again. The story. City traffic hummed somewhere over neighborhood rooftops. Invisible cicadas sounded from the trees.

The phone rang faintly in the distance. She hurried inside. Her husband, wanting to know if she'd meet him for an early supper. Yes, that'll be fine. She set the phone down, leaving her hand upon the ringer. As if she might call him back. Or someone else. As if she might now make some call weighing down on her. Some call she'd never made before. To some person that mattered to her heart.

In the studio she sat backwards on a chair, resting her chin on the chair's back as she'd done years ago. When young. Several works in progress sat unfinished on their stands, terrains calling to be filled-in, to be given fences and rows of cotton and old barns long since forgotten. For a moment she contemplated adding people to the paintings. Maybe two old men leaning across a fence row, chatting. A little boy playing in the cool dirt under a lean-to.

On a desk in the studio's corner sat a framed picture of a boy and two men, standing in murky floodwater with a limit of mallard greenheads lying on the log before them. She focused, studying their smiles, their faces. It had been a long while since she'd even noticed the picture, as if it had become a fixture as insignificant as the wallpaper, the curtains. Father, husband, son. The woods behind them exactly as described in the story, bottomland oaks and cypresses reaching toward the hard winter sky.

The phone again. It rang twice before she rose and hurried to the kitchen.

"Mama."

"Cole."

"You're not painting, are you? I can call you back."

"No, I'm not doing much of anything to tell you the truth," she said.

"I was just calling to say hello."

"I got your letter. The story, Cole. It was really good."

"I appreciate that, Mama."

"And I knew all the places in Kefalonia you talked about in your letter. You made me miss it so, although I've never gone to the docks at Fiskardo. I'll have to do that, won't I?"

"Yes you will. Mama?"

"Yes."

"Smitty and I went fishing at Moon Lake yesterday."

"You did?"

"Yes."

"And?"

"It wasn't tough, Mama. It wasn't tough at all."

"Well Cole, things pass. Folks heal."

Silence between a mother, a son.

"I'll be in Oxford for the rest of the summer."

"Okay," she said.

"Same place, you know where to reach me."

"Yes."

"Holler at Pop for me."

"I will."

"All right Mama, I better run, I've got to..."

"Cole?"

"Ma'am?"

"I'm glad he lived. The boy lost in the woods. In the story."

"Me too, Mama," Cole said, "I'm glad the boy lived too."